S0-AAF-706

HOT ON THE TRAIL . . .

So his life was on the line again. As it had been countless times since that first Indian attack on the Iowa farmstead long ago. But never before had he maneuvered himself into such a precarious position for such a vacuous—and perhaps fatuous—reason.

For the discovery of the wagon's secret had not changed his motivation in staying with the Montez family. He had no selfish designs on the gold and cared nothing for the Mexican peons of San Parral it was intended to help.

No, it was simply the need to satisfy his carnal lust for the body of a young woman—whose every curve drove him crazy with desire—that had triggered his responses since he first saw her.

He could take the life of a man without compunction. Why could he not take the body of a woman without consideration for the object of his desire?

WARNING

This story is not for
the faint-hearted reader.

The Edge Series:

WRITE FOR OUR FREE CATALOG

If there is a Pinnacle Book you want—and you cannot find it locally—it is available from us simply by sending the title and price plus 25¢ to cover mailing and handling costs to:

PINNACLE BOOKS
Reader Mailing Service
P.O. Box 1050
Rockville Centre, N.Y. 11571

____Check here if you want to receive our catalog regularly.

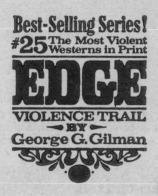

Best-Selling Series!
#25 The Most Violent
Westerns in Print

EDGE

VIOLENCE TRAIL
BY
George G. Gilman

PINNACLE BOOKS   LOS ANGELES

This is a work of fiction. All the characters and events portrayed in this book are fictional, and any resemblance to real people or incidents is purely coincidental.

EDGE: VIOLENCE TRAIL

Copyright © 1978 by George G. Gilman

All rights reserved, including the right to reproduce this book or portions thereof in any form.

A Pinnacle Books edition, published by special arrangement with New English Library, Ltd., London.

ISBN: 0-523-40201-5

First printing, February 1978

Cover illustration by Bruce Minney

Printed in the United States of America

PINNACLE BOOKS, INC.
One Century Plaza
2029 Century Park East
Los Angeles, California 90067

for:

N.P.B.
who welcomed us to a far
plusher place than the one
in Amity Falls.

VIOLENCE TRAIL

Chapter One

ISABELLA Montez watched the lone rider's slow approach and wrinkled her nose against the smell of herself. Her body had been wet with perspiration all morning but she had been aware only of the discomfort. And she had become used to this as one of the many inconveniences and rigors which must be endured on the long and open trail. But never before had her body released the odor which assaulted her nostrils now.

She recognized what it was, though. For her mind was on the brink of panic, her legs seemed about to collapse under her and her hands trembled unless she kept them clenched into tight fists. So, although the blazing sun was close to its midday peak of intense heat, she knew it was the sweat of fear that was drenching her flesh.

The rider was still a half mile out across the Colorado Plateau country, a dark silhouette astride his horse, the outline of man and animal blurred by the shimmering heat haze. The girl crossed herself quickly and even this slight movement seemed to unbalance her. But she reached out a hand to lean on the sideboard of the canted-over Studebaker farm wagon.

"He has seen me and is coming," she said softly and fearfully in Spanish.

1

There was no answer.

The rider had seen her—the distant figure and the tilted covered wagon beside which it stood—as fuzzed by heat shimmer to his eyes as he and his horse were to hers. The man's eyes were blue, the lightest shade of that color, like ice on an ocean at dawn. And their expression upon seeing the girl beside the broken-down wagon was as cold as bleak winter. It had not altered by a part of a degree from when he was on the other side of the mesa, out of sight of what might have been the only other human being in a thousand square miles of otherwise lifeless terrain.

The eyes were representative and the predominant feature of the man's face as a whole. It was a lean face, the eyes mere slits beneath hooded lids. The nose had a hawklike quality between high cheekbones. The jawline was firm, the nostrils slightly flared, the mouth broad and thin. The skin, stretched taut over the bone structure, was darkened by more than exposure to every kind of weather condition, and the lines inscribed deeply into it were not entirely caused by the passing of close to forty years. To each side of the face there was a shoulder-length fall of thick, jet-black hair.

His build was also lean, for his near two hundred pounds of muscular weight was hung on a rangy framework that reached to a height of six feet three inches.

Despite the coldness of his expression and the constant watchfulness of his narrowed eyes—which saw the girl and the wagon as just one other composite feature of the vast landscape stretching away on every side—he rode easy in the saddle of the black mare. It was a good, serviceable Western saddle cinched to the strong back of a good and serviceable Western horse. The man's clothing and gear were equally suitable to

2

riding the high Colorado country and whatever lay beyond, where extremes of weather might be just one brand of danger. A wide-brimmed, low-crowned black Stetson; a sweat-stained gray kerchief loosely knotted and not quite concealing a beaded leather thong that encircled his neck; a gray shirt, also sweat-stained, buttoned at the wrists; and black denim pants with the cuffs outside unfancy, down-at-heel riding boots. No spurs.

Around his waist there was a worse-for-wear gunbelt slotted with shells. The holster, tied down to his right thigh, held a .45 Frontier Colt. A lariat was hung on one side of his saddle. On the other was a rifle boot in which rested a Winchester repeater, a standard model, like the Colt.

Lashed in place at the rear of the saddle was a bedroll. On top of this was a shabby but warm coat. Inside the roll were the few essentials a man needed to prepare, cook and eat a meal.

Inside his saddlebags and canteens there was enough of what he needed until an opportunity came for him to replenish his supplies.

Isabella Montez could see him more clearly now, moving slowly against the slick mirage of heat shimmer rather than through it. She saw details—the dust clinging to the clothing of the man and the coat of the horse, the darkness of bristles on the man's lower face, more pronounced along the top lip and at each side of the mouth to suggest that he favored a moustache.

The girl's fear heightened. She was sweating so much that she felt as if her fully clothed body was immersed in a pool of warm water. The air she breathed seemed to scorch her nostrils and sear the delicate lining of her lungs. She wanted to reach out for the support of the wagon again, but discovered she could not

3

move her arms. She had to will her legs to remain rigid.

She saw the face of the man as ugly—her panicked mind rejecting the basic structure of the features as a whole—seeing only the glittering, dispassionate eyes and the thin, cruel line of the compressed lips.

He halted his horse fifteen feet away from her, level with the rear of the wagon. She caught her breath and terror misted her vision so that the heat shimmer seemed to swoop in and make the figures of the man and his horse indistinct again.

It was a slight movement of the man's left hand, releasing the reins, which startled Isabella. The hand continued to move, traveling up to briefly grip the brim of his hat with a thumb and forefinger. The lips, no longer pressed together, had parted to display very white teeth in a smile that drew nothing from the eyes.

"Buenos dias, señorita," he said in perfect, unaccented Spanish.

Just as she had seen the menace which lurked beneath the nonchalant facade of the man, so he had become aware of her much more obvious fear of him. He did not reveal his surprise that the use of Spanish served only to expand her terror. He dropped his hand to the reins and closed down the smile.

"Guess it's one lousy day for you, lady," he growled in English. "Real frightful, uh?"

The girl continued to stare up at him, the expression of alarm frozen on her dark-skinned, very pretty face. Perhaps there were tears mixed in with the beads of sweat crawling across her cheeks. He neither knew nor cared.

He tugged gently on the reins and tapped his heels against the mare to steer the animal around the petrified girl.

4

Perhaps it was a sudden shift of her eyes away from his face. Perhaps it was a sense of the presence of a third party. Perhaps it was a slight creaking sound just discernible above the clop of the horse's slow moving hooves. Whatever it was that warned the man of danger came too late.

He had time to streak his right hand from the reins and fist it around the butt of the holstered Colt. As part of the same action, he turned from the waist to look at the rear of the canted wagon.

He saw the head and shoulders of a man. No, a boy. Mexican features, showing a strong family resemblance to the girl. In the same youthful age group as her. Afraid, but controlling his jangling nerves. Using the adrenaline to give extra impetus to his move, allying it coolly with his skill.

The lariat was already snaked out against the pure blueness of the midday sky. The coil was held loosely in the boy's left hand while his right gripped tightly around the main line. The loop was wide enough to take account of any move the man on the horse had time to make.

For the shortest instant, the scene seemed as frozen as the terrified expression on the girl's face. Then the braided rawhide loop dropped. The boy chose precisely the right moment to jerk on the main line. The spliced honda hissed along the rope and the loop dug hard into the flesh of the man's forearms, trapping them against his hips.

There was no chance to draw the Colt, just time enough to kick his feet clear of the stirrups. Then the boy braced a shoulder against the rear bow of the wagon and hauled on the rope.

The man was tipped backwards out of his saddle.

"Es formidable!" the boy yelled, baring yellow teeth in a broad grin.

The black mare scuttled forward. The man was wrenched backwards. The horse halted and looked around balefully. The man hit the ground hard on his rump, the impact at the base of his spine transmitting the jarring effect to every bone in his body.

The boy jerked again on the main line and the man was forced to go out full length on his back as his captor leapt over the tailgate of the wagon. The boy kept the rope bowstring taut.

"Yeah, you're terrific, kid," the man rasped through clenched teeth. "But I hear tell the good die young."

The boy's grin became a sneer as he shortened the main line into the coil, advancing quickly and never allowing slack in the rope.

"El fusil, Isabella!" the youngster ordered, halting three feet away from his prisoner, leaning backwards to keep the rope in a rigid line.

Terror ebbed from the girl, but her hands were trembling as she fumbled to draw the Winchester from the boot.

"Either kill me with it or don't point it at me, lady," the man warned evenly. "Give folks the one warning. You've had yours."

The boy moved with agile speed. He took a step forward, stooped, released the lariat with one hand and crashed a fist into the point of the man's jaw.

The man experienced agony. The sky changed from blue to black. The girl, the boy and the crippled wagon were gray shadows against the blackness. Somebody voiced an obscenity. It took two seconds for him to realize he had cursed. Color came back to the world. The pain diminished but was still there. His right hand was cupped over an empty holster.

6

No, much longer than two seconds. The colors were the same, but the figures had changed position against the land and sky. He was sitting upright, his back against the spokes and rim of a wagon wheel. His arms were held to his side by more than one loop of rope. Spare rope held him fast to the wheel. His ankles were tied together by a kerchief. All this could not have been achieved in two seconds. The boy threw a punch as effectively as a rope.

The man cursed again.

"I give you a warning, *hombre*," the boy snarled. "Isabella is my sister and I do not like for her to hear such language. You say once more, and I cut out your tongue. I lose no sleep over such a thing."

They were squatting on the ground some ten feet in front of him. With the time to survey them at greater length and in close proximity, the man thought they were twins. Nineteen or twenty years old, matching heights at about five feet nine inches and both weighing around a hundred and thirty pounds.

Isabella was growing out of youthful prettiness towards mature beauty and the transition stage was easy on the eye. Her dusky features were perfectly formed within a framework of highly sheened black hair that reached way below her shoulders in a series of natural waves. Her forehead was high, her eyes dark and clear and large, her nose petite and her mouth poutingly full. She was dressed in a Stetson, denim shirt and pants, and high-heeled riding boots. All blue and the worse for wear. The shirt and pants fitted snugly to a body that was a little heavy—full, but firm-looking.

"And do not look at my sister like that, *hombre!*" the boy snarled.

He seemed slim by comparison with Isabella but his

tight-fitting garb—identical to that of the girl with the addition of a black vest and a gunbelt—contoured a build that contained a great deal of strength. But, even when he glowered in deep-felt anger, his handsome face retained an impression of callow youthfulness.

The man's Colt was in the boy's holster. There was s sheathed knife on the opposite hip. The man's Winchester rested across the boy's knees.

"Or you'll cut out my eyes, kid?" the man asked evenly.

He was sweating hard. So were the two youngsters. But fear, defeat, and triumph were things of the past now. It was simply the heat which squeezed salty beads from wide pores, to trickle across exposed flesh and paste clothing to skin.

The sun had inched just fractionally beyond its highest point. It blazed down with blistering intensity—dazzling yellow against bright blue—on the muted reds, neutral grays and somber greens of rearing ridges, dusty soil and sparse vegetation. At the center of this barren landscape on the Continental Divide, its borders veiled by the shimmering heat haze, was the covered wagon with a broken off-side rear wheel. Two oxen were still harnessed to the draw pole. The man's black mare—saddled and with the bedroll in place—was hitched to the tailgate. The animals flicked their tails at the irritation of buzzing flies. The captors used their hands as ineffective swats. The captive endured this additional discomfort without any sign that it bothered him.

"That, too, I might do, *hombre!*"

"Pedro will do nothing of the kind," the girl said wearily and ignored his glower as she continued to look at the man. "But he will kill you if he has to."

Perhaps she had been close to exhaustion before the

8

lone rider approached. Or maybe the experience with terror had drained her of vitality. The dullness in her eyes and her soft-spoken voice acted to add extra menace to the simply stated threat.

Pedro forgot the put-down and spread a grin of triumph across his face again. "It will be very easy, *hombre*."

The man parted his lips to show the thinnest of wry smiles as he made a token attempt to strain against the tightly tied rope. "Figure I'm bound to agree with you, kid."

"He is not afraid of us, Pedro,'" Isabella said in the same dull tone as before. But there was a faint expression in her eyes now as she continued to watch the lean, darkly bristled face which was only partially shaded by his hat brim. Curiosity and doubt or a mixture of the two. "He simply accepts that he has lost and we have won. Why do you not accept this without crowing like the victor in a *riña de gallos?*"

This drew another angry glower from her brother and again she did not look at him. She merely sighed, as if she were used to rebuking him in vain.

"Perdón!" the boy snapped with heavy sarcasm and thrust upright. *"Voy a——."*

"He speaks our language as well as we do," his sister interrupted.

Pedro made a sound of disgust. "And I have no wish to speak to him in any language! I will keep watch. You do whatever you want to!"

He began to amble in a slow, ill-tempered patrol line around the canted wagon, peering into the shimmering distance and gripping the Winchester tightly in two hands across his flat belly.

"Does he have enough guts to kill a hog-tied man, *señorita?*"

9

"I do not know. And it does not matter. It will be the decision of our father when he returns from Amity Falls with the new wheel. And our father will do whatever it is he feels is necessary."

There was no defined trail in any direction across this strip of high country. The wagon had left signs to show it was heading due south. The black mare had impressed hoofprints in the dust from the northeast. Other signs showed that two horses had been ridden away from the crippled wagon, their destination lying southwest.

"He as short-tempered as his son?"

"As determined to return to San Parral, *señor*. But a good man and wise. Pedro is good. One day, perhaps, he will learn wisdom."

The boy heard this and muttered under his breath.

"No, lady, the name means nothing to me," the man rasped, catching the sudden intensity of the girl's gaze when she mentioned San Parral. "Same way you and your brother meant nothing until he roped and clipped me."

Isabella, weary and dejected again, shifted eyes to peer out along the tracks left by the mare. "I saw you come around the mesa. Pedro was inside the wagon. We agreed on the plan. He was excited. I wanted you to leave us alone. You rode directly to us. Perhaps to offer help. But we trust no one." She returned her attention to the lean, deeply scored face with the cruel mouthline and slitted, glittering eyes. "There is some blood of Mexico in your veins, *señor*. It can be seen in your features. And you speak the language of Mexico better than many full-blooded Mexicans."

"When did they make that a crime, lady?"

She chose to ignore the wry comment.

"You have the look of a man not to be trusted,

10

señor. And it is not only the weapons you carry which make you appear a *pistolero*." She shook her head. "I'm sorry. A man cannot help the way he looks."

"Or the way he looks at a woman like you."

She came erect, and winced as a small bone in her leg cracked. "You are not stupid enough to believe you can win my sympathy with flattery, *señor?*"

"Just telling you the way it is with me, Isabella. Been a long, tough ride, uh? And still a long way to go? San Parral's in Mexico? I ain't out to win anything. What are you and your folks betting on?"

She half turned to peer towards the southwest, using both hands to supplement the shade of her hat brim. "If my father believes you do not know, then it is no business of yours, *señor*."

There was concern in her tone.

"He's been gone a long time?"

A nod. "With my mother. Since early morning. Do you know how far it is to Amity Falls?"

"Don't know a thing about this part of the country. Nor the people in it. Any of the people."

"It is my father who will need to be convinced."

"Isabella, tengo hambre!" her brother called, maintaining his despondent patrol around the wagon.

"I will prepare a meal," the girl told the man. "It will be cold. My father warned against fires. There are Shoshone Indians in the area. You will eat with us. It will not be a feast."

The man nodded. "There sure ain't anything to celebrate, lady."

Despite the fact that he was securely bound, she circled wide around him to climb up over the tailgate of the wagon.

"Hey, *hombre,* what's your name?" Pedro asked after walking his sentry route twice more, then halting on the spot vacated by his sister.

"Edge," the man answered. He had closed his eyes when the girl went from sight. He did not open them now.

"Edge? That is not a Mexican name. It was your mother who was Mexican?"

"Father, kid."

"Then how come you're called Edge, *hombre?*"

"It's a long story. And you and your sister've got troubles enough of your own without listening to mine."

Pedro gave a short, hollow laugh. "Okay, *hombre*. If it turns out we have to kill you, we'll just put that name on the marker."

"Stop this talk of killing," Isabella snapped, "and take these."

She thrust two tin plates over the tailgate of the wagon. Pedro rested the Winchester reluctantly on the ground and complied with the order. He placed one plate beside Edge and retreated to where the rifle lay. The meal was comprised of cut up jerked beef, beans, and a chunk of sourdough bread. There was a spoon to eat it with and Pedro shoveled the food greedily into his mouth.

"I will feed you or you will go hungry, *Señor* Edge," the girl stated. squatting down close to the prisoner with a plate of her own. "You must remain tied."

She had brushed her hair and wiped the old sweat from her face. And used too much cheap perfume to mask the muskiness of former fear.

"A little slower than your brother takes it," Edge said. "I'd hate to disappoint him and choke to death."

The girl was herself eating as discreetly as the conditions and implements allowed.

12

"*Hombre!*" the boy snarled. "You will not talk so tough when my father gets back."

Beans and crumbs of bread were showered from his mouth as he voiced the new threat.

"Finish your food and get back to watching for Indians," his sister countered.

The weariness was back in her tone but her words had the same effect as if she had shrieked them at Pedro. The only outward sign of his disgruntlement was a childlike sullenness.

"From up on the wagon seat." Edge suggested. "It ain't much, but any kind of height is better than nothing in open country."

"Concern yourself with your own business, *hombre!*" the boy rasped, wiping his plate clean with a final piece of bread and thrusting it into his mouth.

Edge chewed on a chunk of beef the girl had spoon-fed him. "You laid claim to my tongue and eyes. kid," he allowed in a growling tone. "Means my scalp is still up for grabs. Sooner it wasn't a Shoshone brave got his hands on it."

Pedro resumed his guard duty, tossing his plate and spoon into the rear of the wagon as he passed. After one and a half circuits, he climbed up onto the front of the wagon and stood erect on the seat.

Isabella continued to eat and to feed Edge. Twice, her light brown face became flushed as her gaze was trapped from its wandering by the ice blue eyes of the man. After that, she worked hard at looking everywhere except directly into the glittering slits beneath the hooded lids. But then the silence, marred only by the monotonous buzzing of the flies, got to her.

"I am terribly afraid that we may have made a mistake about you, *señor*," she blurted out, her voice low,

13

as if she did not want her brother to hear the admission.

"Figure you've gotten used to being that," Edge answered.

"Mistaken?"

"Afraid. What's in the wagon? A million dollars worth of family heirlooms?"

She caught her breath, looked sharply at his impassive face, then away again.

"I ain't a thief, lady," he added, watching the pulse at the side of her throat reveal how fast her heart was beating. "Nor a rapist if that's something else that's bothering you." He turned his head to scowl briefly along the side of the wagon. "I just might give your brother something to remember me by. But he'll live."

When he returned his attention to her, Isabella had gathered up the soiled utensils and pulled herself erect. From his low angle, looking up the profile of her body, the curves of hips, belly and breasts were almost painfully sexual in silhouette against the bright sky.

"I'm sorry," she whispered. "It is for our father to decide."

She spun around and her quick movements in walking to the rear of the wagon and climbing up over the tailgate served to emphasize her fully blossomed sexuality.

"The eyes, *hombre!*" Pedro called, leaning out from the side of the wagon to stare menacingly down at the prisoner.

"I got no complaint about those, either," Edge muttered, moving his head so that the top of the wheel rim tipped his hat forward lower over his forehead.

Inside the wagon, Isabella made small noises cleaning the plates and spoons. The flies maintained their constant buzz, alighting and taking wing. Soon, Edge

14

could hear only the flies and his own regular breathing as background noise to his thoughts. Vague, lethargic thoughts about his latest troubles in a troubled life. Shallow thoughts which kept chasing each other around in endless circles. An apparently useless exercise in which another kind of man may have indulged to keep at bay anxiety about his fate. But this man had learned from many harsh lessons that it was futile to worry about the outcome of any situation over which he had no control. So he contemplated his predicament in order to keep his mind off the nubile body of a woman half his age.

Until a new sound abruptly emphasized his helplessness and flooded more sweat from every pore in his flesh. At the same time, fear seemed to contract his insides into a small, tight, ice-cold ball at the pit of his stomach.

There had been the creaking of a board in the bed of the wagon. A familiar enough sound. But, this time, it disturbed from lethargy a coiled diamondback snake which had been sleeping in the shade of the crippled vehicle. And it was the rattle of anger from the vibrating tail of the creature which triggered the half-breed's fear.

Isabella gasped. Then she rasped, "Pedro!"

The boy had heard the rattler, too. "Hey, *hombre!*" he called lightly, looking along the side of the wagon and grinning. "Maybe this will decide it for you before the return of *mi padre,* eh?"

The girl was looking down at Edge from the rear of the wagon, the horror inscribed into her face, making her look like a small child.

The half-breed moved just his head, to lift the hat brim up from over his eyes. Then turned slowly from the neck to gaze at the four feet long western diamond-

15

back slithering from out of the shade into the bright sunlight. The reptile's anger at being aroused was gone. The only sound it made was a low, rasping one caused by the friction of its flesh against the dust. Its yellow eyes gleamed and its jaws were wide, the forked tongue constantly extending and retracting between bright fangs.

"It's like the Garden of Eden, is it not, *hombre?*" Pedro Montez taunted. "Adam tempted by Eve. Now we have *el serpiente.*"

Edge's vision was misted by the beads of sweat which dripped off his forehead and splashed onto the hooded lids of his narrowed eyes. The rattler was six feet away and slithering slowly closer. Cautiously curious now, perhaps seeing the unmoving man as a newer, more comfortable place to coil up against and sleep. The half-breed curled back his lips and spoke in a rasping tone through his clenched teeth.

"It ain't an apple that's about to get bit, kid." It was a struggle to keep his breathing shallow.

"Pedro, you must—"

She was staring at her brother along the side of the canted wagon. Edge altered the direction and focus of his own gaze.

The boy nodded, and his grin of pleasure was momentarily replaced by a scowl of disappointment. Then, as he took his right hand away from the Winchester and reached across the front of his body to draw the knife from the sheath, intent concentration showed on every plane of his face.

The rattler was within twelve inches of exploring Edge's thigh with the darting tongue. A muscle spasmed involuntarily in the man's leg. Most of the stocky length of the snake became immobile. Only the tail moved, trembling fast to sound the staccato warn-

16

ing of dangerous fear. Then the head rose, jaws gaping to their widest extent, drops of venom beaded at the needle sharp tips of the fangs.

The boy drew back his right hand at shoulder height, then hurled it forward. The knife spun free of his grip, rotating glinting blade over matt black handle. The point dug into the body of the snake just behind the bulge of the head. The jaws snapped closed, then sprang open again. The point of the knife broke clear of flesh. The snake folded double and rolled. Then extended to its full length and writhed in death throes. Its jaws continued to open and close in time with the agonized contortions of its body. The sound of its rattle seemed to fill the entire world. Then it became still and silent on a deathbed of disturbed dust.

"Obliged, kid," Edge said, blinking sweat off his eyelids. "Figure that wipes the slate clean between us."

"*Sí, Pedro,*" Isabella gasped. "*Gracias. Muchas gracias.*"

"*De Nada,*" her brother replied with heavy sarcasm. He swung down to the ground and moved forward to stoop and pick up the snake. He examined the dead reptile with keen interest, then withdrew his knife, replaced it in the sheath without cleaning the blade, and dropped the corpse. He laughed, flicking his gaze from Edge to Isabella and back to the dead rattler. "Adam, Eve and the serpent," he said, relishing the analogy. He crooked a thumb and stabbed it against his chest. "Does that make me God?"

Isabella grimaced. "You are the son of Antonio Montez," she countered flatly, peering out towards the southwest.

Edge and her brother looked in that direction, too. Far away, indistinct in the heat shimmer, two riders could be seen making slow progress with a burden that was slung between their horses.

Pedro shrugged. "No matter. To you, it makes little difference, *hombre*. My father becomes God to you, with the decision of whether you will live or die in his hands."

"Now he's Jesus Christ," Edge muttered, craning his neck to look up at the girl as Pedro returned to stand on the wagon seat.

Isabella responded to his vaguely humorous look with an expression of anxious sadness. "You would do well not to blaspheme, *señor*," she warned, "for my father is deeply religious and quick to anger."

"Like God, his wrath is great!" Pedro taunted bitterly.

"Do not profane the Trinity," the girl urged vehemently. "Ignore my brother, *señor*, and—"

"The son don't bother me, lady," Edge muttered, shifting his gaze away from her to look out towards the riders, who became more clearly defined as they drew closer. "But from what I've heard, I ain't gonna get to love the father."

"I will pray for you, *señor*."

Her brother spat into the dust. "I pray he will kill you, *hombre*."

"If he does, kid, you'll all get haunted by a very damn unholy ghost."

Chapter Two

ANTONIO Montez was a big man. Six feet tall, Edge guessed as he watched the Mexican dismount. Broad at the shoulders and wide at the hips. Too thick around the waist, maybe, but the extra weight would stay firm and muscular for as long as the man remained active.

He was over fifty and if any of his years had been easy ones, he showed no signs of it. There was the dirt of trail dust ingrained into the leather-textured, dark skin of his face. That every trail before this one had been hard to tread and survive was also plain to see in his squinting eyes, misshapen nose and set of his mouth.

Edge looked up at the man standing over him and wondered if he were seeing a reasonably accurate image of himself in years to come. If he lived that long.

Montez and his wife had not quickened their pace as they came close enough to the crippled wagon to see that all was not as they had left it. The woman, who looked older and was bulky with fat rather than muscle, had merely remained in the saddle, patiently awaiting the outcome, as her husband slid to the ground and asked a single question.

He spoke in his native tongue, his tone flat. "What is this?"

Isabella climbed down from the wagon, listening

anxiously as her brother replied from his vantage point. The boy gave an accurate account of Edge's approach and capture and gave it bias only by the obvious dislike in his voice. His father listened attentively, fingering one of his gray sideburns and using a toe of a boot to toy with the dead snake.

"We perhaps acted hastily, Father," Isabella said quickly when Pedro was through. "He did nothing— said nothing against us. It is just that he looks like— like a—"

"A man who would be hard to trust," her father finished for her, then sighed and looked up at his son. "Get the wheel off the horses, Pedro. Isabella, your mother and I have not eaten since we left here this morning."

The youngsters hurried to comply with the requests, the girl climbing back into the wagon while the boy jumped to the ground, rested the Winchester, and went to the horses. He helped his mother from the saddle and then began to untie the ropes which held the mint-new wagon wheel between the animals.

"What are you doing here, *Señor* Edge?" Antonio asked flatly as his wife stepped up alongside him and looked dully at the half-breed. "I regret the need to ask about your business."

The woman was a head shorter than he was. Perhaps she had been beautiful once, but the hard years had wrinkled her skin and soured her expressions. She was garbed in a shapeless and shabby black dress and kept the sun off her sparse, very gray hair with a dirty white mantilla of lace which may have cost a lot of money a long time ago. She dragged her feet through the dust when she walked and, in repose, her head hung low.

"I'll tell you just the once, feller," Edge said evenly

20

in English, looking back to the man, who was dressed poorly in Western style, his clothes owing nothing to Mexico. "This trip I'm out of Nebraska heading southwest. Where I'm going and what I'm going for ain't none of your business. Your wagon and your kids happened to be right in my way. But I was ready to ride on around them. Until my plans got changed."

Antonio wore an old .36 Griswold six-shot revolver stuck into his belt on the right hip, a brass-framed copy of the Colt Dragoon made for the Confederacy. The man cupped a hand over the wooden butt plates, then turned and went to his horse.

"You are going to kill him, Father?" Pedro asked eagerly as he rolled the wheel through the dust.

"You disgust me," his father said wearily, and drew a Sharps rifle from his saddle boot.

"Father!" Isabella exclaimed, leaning from the rear of the wagon with a food-laden plate in each hand.

The man ignored both his children, returning to the place where his shadow fell across Edge, and thumbing back the hammer of the rifle. It was one of the Beechers Bible models, as ancient and ill-cared for as the handgun. Like the man himself, and his wife.

"A bullet in the heart from this, *señor,* and you will tell nobody anything any more. Not even once. I think you are not in a position to dictate terms."

Edge was stiff from being in the same enforced sitting posture for so long. The kid had scared him with the rope. The rattlesnake had been more terrifying. The heat of the day felt as if it had lasted a lifetime.

But hard-learned lessons are not easily forgotten. And he recalled now, even as his temper began to fray, that anger, unless it is coolly controlled, can be fatal. He had survived often by applying this tenet and had come close to death more than once when he ignored it.

21

So he kept his expression neutral and his voice even. "You're a family that talks a lot about killing. So far, all that's dead is a rattler."

"You think I will not kill you, if it proves necessary, *señor?*"

Every Montez was in front of Edge now, Pedro having leaned the new wheel against the broken one and Isabella down from the rear of the wagon, still holding the plates. Now, she seemed as resigned to the results as her mother. The boy was making a poor effort at controlling his excitement. Antonio looked as if the burden of responsibility weighed heavily on his broad shoulders.

"All it takes is the guts to squeeze the trigger, feller," the half-breed allowed. "And I figure you got the guts."

"As you would have in my position, *señor*. But I need something else. A reason. In this case, a belief that you mean us harm." He shrugged, almost imperceptibly. "But there is no way this can be proved. So I must be influenced by my impression of you. I regret, *señor*, it is not a good impression."

Edge nodded, as prepared to die as he always was, accepting the possibility of sudden and violent death as a calculated risk of the kind of life that had been thrust upon him. "I'm having some regrets of my own, feller. But I'll be through with them soon. Yours will last longer."

Antonio nodded in acknowledgement and understanding. "I can only pray that I am taking the—"

He started to swing the Sharps towards the target.

"Stop talking about it!" Isabella shrieked, hurling the plates and their contents into the dust and throwing her hands up to her face. "If you have to do it, do it!"

Antonio's wife raised her head and there were tears

22

in her eyes. Through them she seemed to be expressing a plea for understanding.

Pedro was breathing fast, his youthful face dripping with the sweat of excitement.

The man with the Sharps was as impassive as the helpless prisoner at his feet.

Isabella did not trust herself to keep her eyes covered and closed. She whirled around and put her back to Edge.

The half-breed's resignation to the inevitable death that would come from a large-caliber bullet in his heart was total. Anger was completely gone. And there was not even the cold ball of fear in the pit of his stomach. Instead, he could look out from under his hooded eyelids, see the rigid stance of the young girl and feel the stirring of sexual arousal.

Isabella could not keep her eyes closed. She stared out through the bars of her fingers from eyes misted by emotion. A sob was caught in her throat and she thought she was going to choke. She blinked and swallowed. Her vision cleared. Then she flung one hand forward and shrieked, *"Madre de Dios—Indio!"*

Her father, mother, and brother spun around. Edge leaned as far to his right as the ropes allowed, to look between Antonio and Pedro and through the legs of the Montez horses.

For an instant, there was just the one Indian visible, the shape of the brave and his pony distorted by heat shimmer. But then a group of half a dozen or more appeared behind the leader. They were southwest of the wagon, moving slowly along the tracks left by the mounts of Antonio and his wife.

Isabella lowered her hand, then extended it to the side and clasped the hand of her mother. Pedro

23

scuttled across to retrieve the Winchester. He pumped the lever action, unaware he was ejecting a live shell.

"Senalda, Isabella, Pedro!" the head of the family snapped. "Do not be afraid. Perhaps they mean us no harm."

The party of seven or eight Shoshone braves rode closer, closing in on the crippled wagon. There was no aggression in the manner of their advance. But their pace and silence generated a strong sense of menace. It hovered around them like a palpable part of the dust rising from under the unshod hooves of their ponies.

"Do I get a last request?" the half-breed asked evenly in English.

"Shut your mouth, *hombre!*" Pedro snarled.

Edge ignored him. "Sooner take a bullet from your gun, Montez, than be tied up when those braves get here—maybe with something more in mind than passing the time of day."

Pedro snapped his head around to show the contemptuous grin on his handsome face. "Ah, so you are not made of iron, *hombre*. Death frightens you."

"No, kid. Not death. Just the process of dying."

"Father?" Isabella blurted as her brother rejoined the rest of the family in staring towards the Shoshone advance.

"Antonio," Senalda added in the same pleading tone. "The man is not even all *gringo*. And even if he was not the son of a Mexican father he would surely be with us against a common enemy."

The broad-shouldered, gray-haired man did not reply for a long time. He and his family were as still as the unmoving half-breed, not caring about the irritating flies which buzzed around their ears and crawled across their sweat-run flesh.

The Indians were less than a quarter of a mile away

24

now. And their poverty could be seen in the way their ragged shirts and torn pants hung on emaciated frames, in their disease-scabbed and filthy faces and in the underfed and unkempt condition of their ponies. The leader sat in a saddle. The others rode bareback or on blankets. Each rode with one hand on rope reins. In the other hand, each held a rifle.

"I cannot ask a man I do not trust to give me his word of honor, *señor*," Antonio Montez said at length. "But if any of my family are to survive, it will be seen whether or not I almost made a tragic error of judgment. Cut him free, Pedro."

"But, Father, what if they mean us no—"

"The belt of the brave heading up this bunch, kid," Edge interrupted. "What's hanging from it ain't beaver pelts."

The boy leaned forward, narrowing the gap another few inches as the Shoshones halted their advance and steered their ponies into a line facing the wagon and the whites.

"*Si, Pedro*," his father augmented. "The Indians have claimed scalps."

His wife moaned. Isabella gasped, snatched her hand away from her mother's grip and ran to Pedro. As she reached for the handle of his sheathed knife, the boy whirled away from her.

"I will do it! And I will watch him as closely as I watch the Indians."

He crouched beside Edge, drawing the knife and first cutting through the kerchief at the half-breed's ankles.

"And maybe you can do it, kid," Edge growled, feeling the pressure of the rope around his body ease as the blade was sawn back and forth. "You do a lot of

25

talking through your ass. Maybe you got eyes back there as well."

The Shoshone braves watched stoically, their heads protected from the blistering sun only by matted black hair held off their impassive faces by rawhide bands. Antonio, Senalda and Isabella Montez returned the unblinking stares with mounting apprehension.

"First the snake, now the Indians, *hombre*." Pedro rasped as the final strand of restricting rope was severed. "Twice I give you a new chance to live. I would expect—"

From the neck down, Edge was stiff from the long period of enforced idleness. There was even pain where the tightness of his bonds had cut through his shirt and impaired his circulation. The pain became intense and forced a groan through his clenched teeth as he powered into sudden movement.

His right arm folded up from the elbow as his left streaked across the front of his body. Both hands fisted around the barrel of the Winchester. Pedro, off-guard as he pushed the knife into his sheath, vented a cry of alarm.

His family snapped their heads around.

Edge had half rolled onto his right hip. Now he went into another roll to the left.

Pedro's cry became a snarl of anger as the rifle was wrenched from his one-handed grip. He started to come erect, drawing the knife out of the sheath again.

The half-breed's left elbow cracked against the ground. The entire length of the arm seemed to be on fire with agony. But he used it as a lever to rock into a second roll to the right.

The boy had the knife clear of the sheath and was swinging it high.

26

Edge raised the elevation of the back-to-front Winchester.

The two women were screaming, their shrill voices masking the words which Antonio Montez was yelling.

Pedro's knife hand started forward, in a downward stabbing action. The stockplate of the rifle crashed into his wrist. The sound of the boy's anger became shriller, then changed abruptly to a scream of pain as his hand was crushed between the rifle stock and the side of the wheel rim.

"Always expect the unexpected, kid," Edge growled as the knife fell to the dust. "Ain't no formula for a life of happiness, but it can cut down on the grief."

He made no attempt to turn the rifle as he shifted his gaze from the tear-stained face of the boy to meet the enraged stare of Antonio.

The women were silent now.

"He stole both my guns, feller. Happy for him to keep the Colt until this is over."

"I would have ensured you were armed, *señor,* if the Indians showed signs of being hostile."

"Obliged for the thought, feller," Edge answered, grimacing at new stabs of pain as he eased upright, using the Winchester and wheel for support. "But, given the freedom, I prefer to take care of my own needs."

"*Bastardo!*" Pedro hissed, rubbing at his injured hand.

"My ma and pa were married, kid," the half-breed rasped. "So don't call me that again. Feel the same way about that word as I do guns aimed at me."

Antonio glowered darkly at his son, angered by the word.

"What are they waiting for?" Senalda rasped fearfully.

27

Her blurted words were accepted by the others as a warning that the potential threat of the Shoshone band was of more immediate concern than the enigma of the tall, lean stranger with the glittering eyes and cruelly set mouth.

"It sure ain't Christmas or a train," Edge muttered.

"Help, perhaps?" Antonio suggested to anyone who cared to comment.

"So why did they show themselves this early, feller?"

"Talk will achieve nothing!" Isabella moaned. "Unless it is with the Indians." She raised her hands to her face and cupped them around her mouth. "You! What do you want? If you want food and water, we have a little to spare!"

The braves remained unresponsive astride their ponies. Their posture was slumped and weary. Had it not been for the bunch of scalps hung at the waist of the leader and the rifles in every hand, the group would have presented an image of pitiful dejection.

"You have experience of dealing with Indians, señor?" Antonio asked, without turning around.

"I've killed a few," Edge replied flatly. He was holding the Winchester across his stomach now, one hand around the frame with a finger curled to the trigger and the other fisted on the barrel.

"And did that teach you anything about them?" the Mexican retorted in a tone of rebuke.

"Yeah. That when they're dead, they can't kill me."

"I do not talk with White Eyes squaw!" the leader of the Shoshones shouted suddenly, drawing himself erect on his pony. "I talk with man who leads you. I say to him to take other men and leave wagon. Go away from there. Squaws stay. We come. Take what we want. Take squaws. Then we go."

Senalda fastened fingers like talons onto her husband's forearm. Antonio growled like a cornered animal. Pedro drew the Colt left-handed. Isabella folded her arms across her breasts, cupping her shoulders with her hands.

"That feller drives a hard bargain," Edge muttered, remaining at the side of the tilted wagon as Pedro stepped forward to stand beside Antonio.

"And one you would accept, were it left to you, *señor?*"

"But it ain't, so we'll never know."

"I wait for your answer, leader of the White Eyes!" the spokesman for the Shoshones demanded.

"Isabella, take the pistol from my belt," Antonio instructed calmly. "When they come close enough, use it. Pedro, you will also hold your fire until they are close."

"I think you will fight, White Eyes!" the Shoshone called. "Your choice! All will die!"

The Indian leader made the first move, releasing his hold on the reins and throwing the stock of his rifle to his shoulder.

Antonio Montez wasted time in compensating for his daughter's reluctance to reach for the old Griswold revolver. He wrenched it clear of his belt and arced it across in front of his wife.

A rifle shot exploded from behind the Montez family. The bullet spiraled out from the muzzle of the half-breed's Winchester, cracked between the shoulders of Antonio and Pedro and buried itself in the heart of the brave on the far right of the line. He, like the other Indians, had aped the actions of the group's leader. His rifle slipped, unfired, from his dead hands as he was tipped backwards over the rump of his pony, the slick patch of wet crimson on his shirt front providing a splash of bright color against the drabness of his shabby clothing.

Seven Shoshones did fire, sending a wide spray of lethal lead towards the group of whites at the side of the wagon.

Edge was already down on the ground, pushing himself backwards with his elbows under the shade and token cover of the wagon.

Isabella had failed to catch the tossed gun and was stooping, with a strangely feminine grace, to pick it up. Antonio fired wildly as he dived full length, dragging his screaming wife with him. Pedro was late in going under the bullets. But he was lucky. Bullets cracked close to him, but not close enough. And, when he went down, it was behind the cover of his father's horse, the animal having dropped like carved rock as blood spouted from two head wounds.

But cover to the front was not enough. For the braves had wheeled their horses and were galloping them on a circular path, stringing them out with wide gaps between. The leader and one other brave had repeater rifles. After the initial fusillade, the other five spaced their shots so that a constant barrage was maintained, despite the need to reload.

In the drifting dust and gunsmoke, the stink of burnt cordite and the cacophony of shooting and shouting, the family of Antonio Montez followed his orders instantly. With bullets thudding into the wagon timbers, ricocheting off the metal work and snagging into the dirt, they scrambled out of the open and under the wagon.

"Front and left!" Edge yelled at the head of the family. "I'll take rear and right."

He exploded a sixth shot and scored only his second hit. A pony, the cannon bone of a right foreleg chipped by the bullet, stumbled and rolled. The rider leapt skillfully clear of the animal. He landed sure-footed and powered into a fast spring towards the wagon.

Pedro fired the Colt and hit only dirt.

"Wait, I told you!" Antonio snarled, fumbling a fresh round into the breech of the Sharps.

Senalda was in a kneeling posture, hands over her ears and forehead pressed to the ground. Her son was on one side of her and her daughter the other. Antonio was at her head and Edge at her heels.

The horseless Indian ran closer. He emptied his single-shot Spencer and vented a shriek of frustration when the bullet went high. He dragged a tomahawk from his belt.

Edge fired another shot and missed his target, galloping at full speed through billowing dust.

"Now, Pedro!" Isabella screamed.

Three shots, in perfect unison and amplified by the close confinement beneath the tilted wagon, drew a high-pitched sound of utter terror from the older woman.

The running brave was stopped in his tracks. And lifted up on to his toes. Then he threw his hands out to the sides, hurling away the tomahawk. He fell in the form of a cross and remained so in the stillness of death. Three areas of slick red on his chest expanded, touched and formed one.

"I got the *bastardo!*" Pedro roared. His voice was high with excitement. Then became a growl as he snapped his head to left and right to glower at his father and Edge. "Alone I would have killed him!"

Antonio nodded and, just for an instant, there was an expression of surprise mixed with pride on the crinkled, sweaty, and dust-smeared face.

"Long as I know, kid," Edge allowed, snapping his

head around as a bullet clanged against an iron wheel-rim.

He pumped the action of the Winchester and fired at the brave who was wheeling his horse for a direct charge at the wagon and swinging the single-shot rifle around his head like a club. The bullet drilled into the center of the filthy forehead. And exited through the top of the skull. The brave dropped the rifle but his nervous system kept his muscles taut. He rode perhaps three yards, a corpse with brain tissue gushing out of the top of his head. Then he crumpled and went backwards off his pony, which veered to the side and galloped away from the gun battle arena.

"Sure shot your idea all to hell, feller," the half-breed growled as the brave bounced to the ground, the impact spewing a fresh gout of gore out of the top of his head.

The Sharps cracked out. A Shoshone screamed. Antonio groaned.

"Father!" Isabella shrieked, lunging across her terrified mother to reach for him.

"I need more shells!" Pedro demanded.

Edge counted four braves still astride ponies. They were still circling, but riding wider on each circuit to spiral outwards from the wagon. Abruptly, they closed up into a group and veered sharply away. Dust rose around them. Gray shafted with yellow sunlight, shrouding them. The beat of unshod hooves galloping became less loud. Senalda curtailed her screams. Isabella sobbed and called to her father softly. There was the sound of a hammer being cocked, a trigger pulled and a firing pin clicking against a spent cartridge case many times.

The half-breed turned his head. He saw that Pedro was up in a crouch, as high as the sloping underside of the wagon would allow. The Colt was thrust out in front of him, gripped two-handed. It was aimed at the diminishing cloud of dust. The face behind the gun was bathed with beads of sweat, but the bared teeth and wide eyes gleamed far more brightly than the moisture. Excitement had also caused more wetness to flow, spreading a dark stain at the crotch of the boy's pants.

"Ain't saying the game's over, kid," Edge said, reaching out to close a fist over the hot barrel of the Colt. "But the opposition called a time out. And you ain't about to score again with an empty gun."

The soft-spoken words broke into the private world which the boy had wrapped around himself. He abruptly surrendered the gun and altered the focus of his eyes from the fleeing Shoshones to his immediate surroundings. First he saw the impassive, stubbled face of the half-breed. Next he became aware of the huddled form of his mother. Then the prostrate figure of his father with his sister demanding that the wounded man show her some sign of life.

He moaned, thrust his mother roughly aside and then became gentle. He spoke placatingly to his sister in Spanish, eased her away and carefully rolled his father over onto his back.

Antonio Montez had taken a bullet in the belly. There was blood in the dust where he had fallen. A great deal more was staining the front of his shirt, spread out wide in every direction from his navel. His eyes were closed, the lids brown in color. The remainder of the deeply lined face was gray, several shades darker than his hair.

Isabella sensed, like her brother a moment ago, that there was a world outside her private thoughts. Her brother spoke softly to their father, stroking his cheeks. She looked away, and saw Edge. The half-breed was taking shells from the left-hand side of his gunbelt and feeding them through the loading gate of the Winchester.

"*Va a—?*" she began, fear trembling her voice and spreading the dullness of resignation across her lovely eyes.

"If he lives, he'll know he almost made a bad mistake, Isabella," Edge cut in. "I never wanted anything from you people."

The Indians were gone. Their own dust had hidden them for most of the way. Now they were beyond the slick-looking curtain of heat shimmer. Edge backed out from under the wagon and straightened. Now that the threat of death had once more receded, he was aware of the painful stiffness in his limbs.

"And so you will not help us now that we need you?" the girl asked. "I cannot blame you."

"We need the help of nobody!" Pedro snarled. "Ride on, *hombre*. Go about your business which is none of ours. And leave us to go about ours."

At last it was Senalda Montez's turn to emerge into reality. Her words and the grief-stricken tone in which she vented them revealed that what she discovered was worse than the waking nightmare she had experienced.

The mother, the son, and the daughter gathered close around the unresponsive form of the father.

Edge went to the black mare and checked the animal was unscathed. Then he slid the fully loaded Winchester into the boot and moved around to the other side of the wagon to examine the broken wheel. It was not a rock or deep rut which had caused the spokes to fracture, merely the strain of traveling too many miles supporting too many heavy loads. His impassive eyes raked over the old Studebaker as a whole. The timbers were holed by termites, rotted by damp or warped by age. In contrast, the metalwork was in good shape. Perhaps it was new. Certainly it had recently received a coat of fresh black paint.

"My father breathes easily," Isabella announced dully as she crawled out from under the wagon and stood up. She smoothed down her blouse, tucking it more tightly into the waistband of her pants, then brushed dust off her hips and thighs. The first action acted to display the contours of her breasts more sharply. The second caused the full, firmly conical mounds to tremble beguilingly. "Perhaps he may live—if we can bring him to the doctor in the town of Amity Falls."

Perhaps it was a measure of the man called Edge that he could glance at the girl and feel again the stirring of carnal desire. But if it was, he felt no self-disgust. Neither did he indulge in wishful thinking or sense hope for a future when the circumstances would be different.

"A three-wheeled wagon won't bring anyone anywhere, lady," he replied. "You want to get your kid brother out from under there to give me a hand?"

"I am not her kid brother, *hombre!*" Pedro countered, emerging from beneath the rear of the wagon. "We are twins. Isabella is one second older than I, that is all."

"Okay, kid," Edge allowed. "But sometimes a second makes a difference. I can't fix the wheel alone."

The boy's temper flared. "You make jokes while my father is dying?"

"He is human, Pedro," the girl said, looking hard at the half-breed. "With feelings. Perhaps it is just an act?"

"He acts well only when killing," the young Montez growled, massaging his bruised right hand.

35

"You and your old man performed pretty well, kid," the half-breed answered, shifting his narrow-eyed gaze out to survey the bullet-shattered and dust-covered corpses of four Shoshone braves. "We sure slayed them."

Chapter Three

IT was an exhausting chore, in the blazing heat of afternoon, to raise the wagon, take off the broken wheel and fit the new one. The women were enlisted to help unload the big Studebaker, then to stack various items of freight beneath it while Edge and the boy used brute strength to inch it upwards.

The sweating half-breed was no longer having lustful thoughts about the body of Isabella Montez. When he gave consideration to anything except the muscle-straining, bone-creaking work in hand, it was concerned with why the boy and girl had reacted so aggressively when he showed up. For there was nothing of any great value among the unladen cargo of the wagon. Mostly it was personal and household chattels, the items old and well cared for. There could have been a large quantity of paper money in one of the two trunks or four valises, but the Montez family appeared no more protective of these than any other item hurriedly off-loaded.

During the fitting of the new wheel, Antonio remained beneath the wagon, a folded coat under his head and a pad of cotton lint strapped to his wound. He was unconscious.

The flies were no longer a problem, having abandoned the living to gather in frantic black masses on the dead, feeding greedily on the fresh blood of Indians and horses.

When the new wheel was securely on the axle, Pedro checked on the unchanged condition of his father and then moved away from the wagon. While his mother and sister loaded the cargo again, leaving a space in which Antonio could lie, the boy examined the dead at close quarters, squatting beside horse carcasses with as much keen interest as he showed in Shoshone corpses.

Edge took a drink from a canteen and watered the black mare. Then, recalling that he may have been unconscious for longer than he thought, he checked his saddlebags and gear. He carried little that was worth stealing, and nothing had been stolen.

"We are a family of four, *Señor* Edge," Isabella said as she climbed wearily down from the rear of the wagon and saw the half-breed complete his search. "We have our faults, like any four people anywhere. But, like you, we are not thieves."

Edge slid his Colt from the holster, turned it upside down and rotated the cylinder to eject the spent shell cases. "You took more persuading than I did, lady."

"We all regret what happened," she answered, hanging her head, then looking to where her mother was stooped over her father in the wagon's shade. "And we have been punished severely for our sins."

The half-breed finished loading the revolver. Then he took shells from a saddlebag and slotted them into his gunbelt.

"Your brother takes his punishment real well."

Isabella looked sadly towards Pedro, who was down on his haunches, peering closely at the brave with a hole in the top of his head. "Sometimes, he can be strange, *señor*. We worry about him. You heard him taunt you when you were helpless. Saw him with the

38

snake. Now this. Pedro has a—a—an unhealthy fascination for death."

"Yeah, I noticed," the half-breed muttered. "Ain't nobody told him it's catching?"

"It is my father's state of health that concerns me now, *señor*. Will you help us get him into the wagon? My mother says there is a doctor in Amity Falls. The town is many miles away and the people there do not like foreigners. But a doctor, he must tend the sick, is that not so?"

"Please, *señor*," Senalda called. "Do us this final favor. Then go your own way with our blessing for your help."

The woman seemed to have aged ten years since the start of the Shoshone attack. And looked somehow smaller and thinner in her shabby gown. She seemed to be weaker and closer to death than her resting husband.

"Hey, kid!" Edge yelled. "Like I told you people, a dead Indian ain't no more trouble."

Pedro resented the interruption to his study of the corpse. His handsome face wore a scowl as he returned to the wagon. But then his mood changed. He displayed deep concern and careful consideration for his injured father as he and Edge lifted the unconscious man and placed him on a crudely made bed inside the wagon.

Then, at no small cost in effort, he showed a wan, tight-lipped smile and bowed stiffly from the waist. "Our thanks, *hombre*. And our apologies. I am now capable of taking my father's place until he is recovered."

"Ain't enough," Edge said flatly, swinging up into the saddle of the mare and reaching forward to unhitch the reins from the wagon.

39

Inside the Studebaker, Senalda Montez gasped. Isabella looked shocked. Pedro made a low snarling sound and dropped a hand to cup the butt of the Griswold in his holster.

"I'm hoping there's a saloon in Amity Falls, kid. Figure the least you folks owe me is a rye with a beer chaser."

"You are to ride with us?" the girl blurted with excited relief.

Pedro was scowling again, and jerked a thumb against his own chest. "I require to prove to my family that I can take care of them, *hombre*. You have no need to concern yourself with us." —

Edge took the makings from a pocket of his shirt and began to roll a cigarette. "I'm just concerned with me, kid," he replied, and ran the tip of his tongue along the paper. "And the four Indians you didn't get to see close up."

"Pedro!" the woman in the wagon called dully.

The boy ignored his mother's plea, but responded sullenly to the urgings of Isabella.

By the time Edge had finished the cigarette, the surviving horse was hitched to the tailgate of the wagon and the saddle and bedroll had been removed from the dead animal. Pedro took the reins and Isabella sat beside him. The wagon moved off slowly to conserve the energy of the ox team under the blistering sun and to make Antonio Montez's ride as comfortable as possible.

Edge rode at the same pace for most of the time, occasionally moving ahead of the lumbering team or dropping back beyond the rear of the wagon. At first impression, his attitude was casual. But Isabella, who watched him surreptitiously while her brother stared morosely ahead, saw that the half-breed's eyes were

40

hardly ever still between the narrowed lids. And she recognized there was a grim purpose behind the surface nonchalance as his head turned from side to side. Just as when he turned from the waist to look behind him, to where buzzards had ceased to circle against the unbroken blue sky and were now fighting among themselves amid rising dust as they challenged for the tastiest morsels of human and horse meat.

The man was as he had been as he approached the wagon—physically at ease but mentally alert for the first sign of danger.

"You think the Indians will try to avenge their dead, Señor Edge?" she called, to end a long silence which had been marred only by the sounds of their slow progress across the barren plateau.

"No, lady. But there's a chance they could try again for what they missed out on first time around."

Pedro spat over the side of the wagon. "*Sí*, I think they are stupid enough, *hombre*."

"Do you think they are stupid, Edge?" the girl asked, no longer trying to hide her interest in the half-breed.

"Hungry," Edge answered, aware of the girl's attraction to him as he maintained his surveillance of the surrounding terrain. "For food and women."

Isabella shuddered at a mental image.

Pedro snorted. "But mostly stupid, I think." He snapped his fingers. "They could have killed us like that and taken what they wanted. But they were stupid and waited too long."

"Scared of dying and lazy," Edge went on, as if Pedro had not said anything. "Ain't no man lazier than an Indian brave."

"What do you mean, *hombre?*"

"Indians have got a reputation, kid. Well-earned.

41

Lot of whites are scared to hell just thinking about Indians. That bunch tried to trade on their rep. Less tir-
ing if folks just surrender. And cuts down the chance
of getting killed. Maybe they've done it before and got
away with it."

The boy snorted again, and sucked at his bruised
hand for a moment. "They will know next time that we
do not surrender."

"But they're still hungry, kid. And even Indians are
ready to work real hard to fill empty bellies. If it's the
only way."

"I am glad that a man of experience is riding with
us," Isabella said.

The half-breed's slitted blue eyes locked on her wide
brown ones for a moment. Then she flushed with em-
barrassment as his gaze once more traveled over the
womanly fullness of her body.

"Ain't no man so experienced he's not ready to try
something new," he said lightly.

"My sister was thinking of Indians, *hombre!*" the
boy snarled.

Edge showed his teeth in a thin, wry smile. "But
women are known for changing their minds, kid."

The talk finished. Hooves of horses and oxen
clopped against the rock-hard ground beneath a layer
of dust. Wheels turned and aged timbers creaked.
While he continued to rake the country in every direction, all the way to the shimmering curtain of heat haze
veiling the horizons, Edge thought of other women and
other Indians.

His blonde-haired, blue-eyed, fair-skinned Swedish
mother on the Iowa farmstead. There had been Indian
trouble then, of a minor nature compared with what
was to come. But to the young Josiah C. Hedges, the
occasional raids on the farm by renegade bands of

Sioux had seemed terrifying. As he grew older, he had held a bucking gun in his hand as he helped his Mexican father beat off the attackers, protecting the farm, its crops and its livestock. The man and youth were willing to see all this lost, providing their wife and mother and young Jamie were saved.

When the war came their parents were already dead. Jamie was a cripple and stayed in Iowa to take care of the farm while Josiah went to the battlefields of the east. There were no Indians there, just countless thousands of Confederate soldiers dedicated to killing the Unionist enemy. And six Union troopers who many times came close to murdering Lieutenant, then Captain, Hedges.

The first woman to mean anything to him outside of his mother was the only good thing in the war for the young soldier. Until the body of Jeannie Fisher, upon which he had been introduced to one aspect of manhood, was burned and mutilated and became another casualty statistic.

Then the war was over and the soldier headed back towards the midwest, anxious to become a farmer once more, Jeannie already forgotten. He prepared to put out of his mind everything else which had happened to him during the long, bitter, and bloody battle for a tarnished cause.

But it was not to be.

The six troopers, who had often been a greater threat to him than the Confederates, reached the Iowa farmstead before the ex-captain. They had left it a burning ruin, with the tortured body of Jamie and the corpse of one of their own providing food for the buzzards.

Everything that had happened to him in the war, every lesson he had learned about the art of killing to survive, came to the forefront of his mind. And guided his actions in tracking down and taking revenge against the murderers of his kid brother.

One killing—curiously not of one of the ex-troopers—had resulted in Josiah C. Hedges becoming a wanted man in the state of Kansas. And the name—and man—Edge, had come into being. A man destined to drift across the west, using war-taught skills honed further by experience to survive the constant dangers which either dogged his tracks or lay in wait along the aimless trail.

Apaches had threatened his survival. Mexicans and Americans, too.

Then there had been Elizabeth. A woman who had come to mean more to him, perhaps, than his mother had. They married and for a few short weeks on a farm in the harsh badlands of Dakota, Edge became Josiah C. Hedges again. He discovered there was more to life than mere survival. There was love and hope and ambition.

But there were also the Sioux.

An opening attack warned him. But, although he did not ignore the omen, he did not recall everything which had been taught so harshly during the War between the States and its cruel aftermath.

And Beth died. An awful death. And the same fate which had made him a wanted man for killing a man who meant nothing to him, took another brutal twist. His wife's death had been planned in such a manner that he was made to feel responsible for her terrible end, driving home the lesson he had forgotten. That he was destined to be a loner, forever denied the opportunity to enjoy more than mere survival for its own sake.

He buried Beth's body and set out once more on a

44

trail to nowhere, killing when it was necessary and remaining more cold and detached than ever when the opportunity of establishing a human relationship occurred.

Instead, he chose the rewards of big money. He had elected such a course long before, in Mexico. And the prize of ten thousand dollars had been cruelly snatched from him.

This time, it was Indians again. Apaches. And he surrendered to the inevitability of being a loser as well as a loner. Taking what he could get when he could get it—coldly, impassively, even brutally. Submitting to the ultimate tragic result of his involvement without grief, remorse, regret or anger.

Food, drink, a horse, a gun, a bed or a woman.

Charity Meagher had been the last woman he had taken—and the first since Beth. And she had died in the Dakotas, too. On the frozen waters of the Missouri. Unmourned by any who watched her violent end.

There were no Indians on that storm-lashed night. But they had been at Democracy, the Nebraska town which had been Edge's last stopover along the aimless trail. The Sioux again. No woman mattered, or could matter, until he saw Isabella Montez.

"A penny for your thoughts, *señor*."

There was an earnest expression on her pretty and almost beautiful face.

Edge shook his head. "You've got troubles enough. You don't want to buy more."

"Are yours in the past or the future?" the girl asked.

"He has made it plain that his business is not ours, Isabella," Pedro growled.

Edge had no business in Colorado. And nothing planned for the end of the trail he was riding when he happened upon the wagon with the broken wheel. The

45

black mare which had once belonged to a black man had set the southwesterly course. The rider had given the animal its head, passing through isolated communities and halting only once to restock for his needs.

"Past's gone and the future ain't here yet," the half-breed answered evenly, then gazed briefly at the hard-set lines of Pedro's profile. "Right here in the present the only trouble I got is remembering I told the kid the slate was wiped clean."

The boy both spat and snorted.

"Pedro is young, Edge," Isabella placated. "But he is his father's son and perhaps one day will be as wise."

Now Edge spat. "That won't take much effort, lady. To match a feller that sets off for Mexico in a wagon only fit for burning. With no spare wheel. And with just a single-shot rifle and an out-of-date handgun to protect his family."

Both youngsters flared with anger. But it was the girl who got in first with a snarling retort.

"From the far north of Montana we come! With little money to spare! In the cheapest wagon we could buy! Made as strong as my father's skills as a blacksmith could make it! With two spare wheels, both of which we have used! All of us knowing the dangers! All of us agreeing it was time to return to San Parral! Trusting in providence, not guns, to protect us!"

"What you say to that, *hombre!*" Pedro demanded, after nodding vigorous agreement to everything his sister yelled at Edge. "You are not riding in stupid company, you know!"

"Just the under-capitalized kind," the half-breed allowed evenly, rasping the dusty back of a hand over the bristles on his jaw.

The girl's anger subsided. "I like to think that pro-

46

vidence ensured you were with us at the time your guns were needed, *señor*." She showed a wan smile. "So proving our trust in it is well-founded."

"One member of the present company might figure providence don't merit nothing but antitrust, lady," the half-breed replied.

Isabella nodded her head and there was sadness in her big eyes again as she looked at the tall, lean man on the horse. "*Sí, señor.* Just one. I do not know who has suffered most. You or my father. But my father, if he recovers from this new torment, will continue to have faith. I will pray for you."

"Do that," Edge invited, peering hard into the southwest, where smudges of smoke showed above the heat shimmer in the foothills of some high ridges. "Could just be I'm the answer to a maiden's prayer."

Chapter Four

AMITY Falls did not exude an aura of love and friendship to the newcomers. And the second part of the community's name was also an untruth on this late afternoon. For water merely trickled in meager lethargy down the steeply sloped course into the slow-running stream which formed the town's northern limit.

It was an untidy scattering of crudely constructed buildings of brick, stone, and timber situated on the eastern slope of a hill with a jagged ridge. The sun was already behind the ridge, so that the single-street town was in deep shadow, the early twilight contributing to its somber atmosphere.

The wagon and its escorting rider clattered across a trestle bridge, the height and span of which suggested the stream became a raging river at the time of the spring thaw.

The first buildings were a cautious distance from the watercourse. A general store on one side and a law office and jailhouse on the other. There were wide gaps between a stage line depot, a saloon, a bank, and a livery stable on the same side as the store. Likewise the schoolhouse, church, an office building with several shingles at the entrance, and a meeting hall were set far apart on the other side. Small houses in unkempt gardens were scattered in disarray behind the commercial premises, a well-trodden path from each leading out onto the street.

Also well defined was a trail which followed a line of least resistance up and over the western ridge, to the mining area which was the reason for the town's existence, Edge guessed. For there was nothing immediately apparent in the town itself as to why Amity Falls should be there.

Smoke curled up from every house chimney and there were lights in some windows. On the street, only the Dragonara Hotel and City General Store were open for business. The smoke drifted on mild currents of warm air. The wagon and its escort progressed slowly along the street. Nothing else moved and the silence seemed to have a tangible oppressiveness.

"There," Senalda said anxiously in Spanish, pointing out between her son and daughter. "The building on the right at the end. There is a sign which says a doctor is there."

"It looks dark and empty, Mother," Isabella answered. Then she became aware that Edge was no longer riding beside the wagon. She instructed her brother to halt the team, then leaned to the side to look back. The half-breed had dismounted and was hitching the reins of his horse to the rail out front of the hotel. "You are no longer with us, *señor?*" she called, a little fearfully.

"All Indians ain't lazy!" Edge called back. "Same as all doctors ain't drinking men. Some of them are, though."

"We will wait."

Edge swung open a door, stepped across the wedge of lamplight and closed the door behind him.

"Father is my responsibility," Pedro growled,

49

wrenching over the brake lever and swinging down to the street. "I do not wait for strangers to—"

He was muttering in low-voiced anger. Isabella and Senalda could no longer hear what he was saying as he strutted towards the hotel. The two women glanced anxiously around them at the quiet, unmoving town. And perhaps it was the first chill of evening which caused them both to shudder.

The Dragonara Hotel held no surprises for the half-breed. It was a single story building, as lacking in frills inside as it was out. The saloon section was small, and even given a cramped appearance by a bar counter along the rear and ten tables, each ringed by four chairs. A door in a side wall was labeled with the information: *Rooms this way.*

There were four ceiling lamps, each turned down to half wick. The smell of kerosene was mixed in with the other saloon odors of tobacco smoke, stale liquor, and unwashed bodies. No cheap perfume, though.

A single bartender positioned at a midway point along the counter reluctantly unbent from over a magazine as Edge entered. Two men seated on opposite sides of the table closest to the bartender raised their eyes disinterestedly from the cards of a two-handed poker game and then resumed their concentration on the play. Edge crossed to the unwelcoming bartender.

"Get you something, mister?" the bartender growled, licking spittle from the corners of his mouth. He was fat, fifty, and dull-eyed, dressed in pants and an undershirt crusted with dirt and old sweat.

"Rye and a beer. If your fingers ain't too tired from following the words."

The jibe went over the bartender's head, or he chose to ignore it. "In the same glass?"

"Sometimes. Not tonight."

The beer was drawn, the whiskey poured and both glasses set down in front of Edge.

"Anything else, mister?"

The door from the street was opened.

"Kid would like to know if there's a doctor in the house, feller."

"Doc, you're needed," the bartender said unnecessarily.

"I heard, Barney," one of the card players responded.

"Most urgently, *señor!*" Pedro added, anger bubbling just beneath his anxiety.

Edge turned to look at the two local customers. The doctor was dressed city style, in a suit, vest, and necktie which were all frayed and faded black. He was a short, stockily built man with thin sandy hair and a pale, freckled face. He had the soft hands of his profession and hard-looking green eyes.

"And I need a five or a wild deuce to fill a straight," he went on. "One card, Fred."

"Urgently, I said!" Pedro snarled, and drew the ancient Griswold. His handling of a gun wasn't up to the standard of his roping and knife work. The draw was slow and awkward. And he had the revolver leveled at the back of the seated doctor before he pulled back the hammer. His anger rose to the surface and the gun trembled in his fist.

The doctor was not afraid. He glanced briefly at the boy, then back at his cards without altering his expression of faint eagerness.

"I said one, Fred."

The dealer was in the same mid-fifties age group. Bald, dull-eyed, thick-bodied and smelling of horses. He had holes in his shirt and his pants were patched. He was as unmoved by Pedro's gun as the doctor.

51

The card was taken and the doctor placed it in his hand, his expression the same as before.

"Dealer takes two," Fred announced. "And reckons you didn't make the straight, Doc."

Pedro advanced stiffly between the tables.

The door to the hotel rooms creaked open.

"Beat it, Chink!" Barney snapped.

The door closed again, not all the way.

Edge sipped his beer, narrowed eyes shifting their gaze from the almost closed door, to Pedro, to the card players. And sensed small movements behind him.

"I'm puttin' up two cents that says I got somethin', Fred," the doctor said, pushing the coins into the pot. Then he hardened his tone as Pedro halted two feet behind him, the muzzle of the Griswold almost brushing the sandy hair on the nape of his neck. "And I'm givin' you Mexes fair warnin'. Anyone that's sick'll have to be taken more than a hundred miles to another sawbones. If I ain't around to take care of them, that is. And if you try anythin' with me, boy, you're friend'll be in real bad shape. Too bad for any doctorin', I reckon. With a hole clean through him, back to front."

Edge turned just his head, slowly. Barney was grinning. There were gaps in the expression from missing teeth. He was resting a .52 Starr carbine on the bar top, the muzzle in line with the base of the half-breed's spine.

"Best you aim that thing away from me, feller," Edge muttered.

"Pay two cents to call your bluff, Doc," Fred announced with a sigh, adding the money to the pot. "Got me three of a kind. Two fives and a wild one."

"Rest easy, or rest in peace," Barney told Edge, still grinning.

"You had the warning," the half-breed replied evenly, facing front again. His stance remained nonchalant, but his eyes continued to rake from the group at the table to the cracked open door and back again.

"Didn't want to scare you, Fred," the doctor said, spreading out a natural straight on the table, six to ten. "Ain't that pretty."

"Now you come to attend to my father!" Pedro ordered. "If you do not, I will kill you. For he will die anyway. Unless he is helped at once."

"But live longer than your friend," the doctor pointed out coldly. He cupped a hand over the money in the pot and dragged it across the table to add to the pile of coins in front of him. "Perhaps you had better speak to your impetuous companion, Mex. As one greaser to another."

He had finished speaking before he looked up at Edge. Abruptly, his calm indifference to the situation was gone. He saw the tall, lean half-breed closely for the first time. Perhaps he recognized in the glittering brightness of the slitted eyes and the basic construction of the dirt-grimed and thickly bristled face that Edge was only part Mexican. Or perhaps he was too afraid of the latent menace emanating from the hard-set expression on the face to consider anything less important than saving his own life.

"Barney!" he said, and the word was a croaked plea.

Fred saw the sweat of terror break out on the suddenly trembling flesh of the doctor's face. He started to turn, his chair creaking.

The door in the side wall creaked open another inch. A short, nervous laugh sounded from beyond it.

"You come now!" Pedro ordered, leaning forward to press the muzzle of the old revolver into the neck of the doctor.

Edge whirled to the right, dropping the beer glass and throwing his arm to the side. It was the action of a killer able to recognize to what extent another man was able to kill.

Every man is ready to take the life of another, given the right circumstances. The doctor had looked at the cold anger on the face of Edge and naked terror had sparked his killer instinct. But he had no weapon and there was a gun pressed against his neck.

Barney was alarmed by the abrupt move of the half-breed—the sudden, incredibly fast transition from apparent nonchalance into controlled reflex action. But his first response was to back away.

The right hand of Edge slammed down, trapping the carbine barrel to the bar top for an instant, still aimed at where his back had been a moment before. Then he pushed it at an angle across the scarred wood, as his left hand streaked up to the nape of his neck—and came away even faster.

The bartender only then saw the expression which had terrified the doctor. His grin had evaporated the instant Edge began the move. Now he looked at evil personified in glinting eyes and lips curled back over gleaming teeth. And naked fear created the killer instinct in a small town bartender.

But the Starr was aimed at the table closest to the bar.

Fred vented a groan of anguish and threw himself hard to the floor, tipping over his chair. The doctor might have been a stone statue after a rain shower, unmoving and dripping with sweat as the boy continued to hold the gun muzzle against his flesh.

The space between the bar and the bottle and glass-lined shelves behind was restricted. Barney stepped back farther, and could retreat no more. Saliva ran from the corners of his mouth as he struggled to wrench the carbine free of the half-breed's grip. To his terrified eyes, Edge seemed to grow taller. His left arm, with something that glinted in lamplight protruding from the fist, appeared to stretch like thick elastic.

But Edge was just a man. One who objected to having a gun aimed at him. Part Mexican and angered by those who insulted his dead father's nationality. Intelligent enough to take advantage of the weaknesses in others when his life was on the line.

Thus, he only seemed taller and with a suddenly longer reach to the panicked Barney. In fact, he had used his right hand trapping the carbine to give additional power to his legs. His feet were clear of the floor as his belly slammed across the bar top.

Barney saw the blade of the open straight razor as more than a glint. He saw that it had a point, honed to the same degree of sharpness as the cutting edge. He surrendered his hold on the carbine and raised his hands to cover his face as he tried to lunge to the side.

For part of a second, he had been poised to kill in defense of his own life. The strongest reason of all. But he had been part of the same second late. Now he sought to escape. And again his timing was wrong.

The fist of the half-breed reached the bartender's face before the man's own hands. Barney's mouth was wide, but his throat was too constricted to give vent to a scream. Until the point of the razor penetrated the moist, soft flesh inside the mouth. Then it was Edge's knuckles, hard against the teeth and lips of Barney, which barred the sound. He twisted his wrist and jerked the fist away.

The point of the razor burst through the skin high on Barney's left cheek. Tiny droplets of blood sprayed away from the wound. His scream was strident, then

55

drowned by warm wetness as the razor slashed a tor-renting cut to the corner of the man's mouth.

The shock to his nervous system brought merciful unconsciousness to Barney. But, before he crumpled to the floor behind the bar, everyone in the saloon saw the lower portion of his left cheek flap down to display his gums and surviving teeth awash in a rising flood of bubbled crimson.

Edge unfolded from across the bar and turned around to face the horrified card players and angry Mexican boy. His own expression was impassive again. "The feller didn't pay attention to my warning," he said evenly, flicking beads of blood from the razor before he slid it back into the neck pouch. "Had to give him a sharp lesson."

"Holy cow, Doc!" Fred gasped. "Go see to Barney!"

The door at the side of the fetid and crudely fur-nished saloon opened wide and a figure garbed in a long, flowing white gown and cone-crowned hat emerged.

"Please, sir," the newcomer announced in a high-pitched, whining voice. "I am dedicated to nonviolence. I am a gentle man."

He was an Oriental, both his tone and attitude obse-quious. As Edge looked coldly at him, he thrust his arms stiffly above his head.

"In that outfit, I'll have to take your word you ain't no female," the half-breed growled.

"My father!" Pedro snarled. "He is outside in the wagon. You will come now."

"Go to hell, Mex!" the doctor retorted, starting to rise. "This town takes care of its own first."

Edge had warned the bartender long before he made his move. And Pedro had threatened the doctor. But the boy's response to this latest example of intractability was the more explosively shocking. Certainly more final.

He simply squeezed the trigger of the Griswold. The powder burn of the short range shot was as pungently acrid as the smell of cordite. The doctor died instantly, as the bullet severed the nerves to the brain, punctured the windpipe and blasted the jugular vein before bursting clear at the front of the throat and burying itself at an angle in the table top. The corpse dropped hard down onto the chair, then tipped forward to slump across the table. Coins and playing cards were scattered to the floor.

The Oriental laughed; the sound short and shrill.

Out on the street, Isabella yelled a single word, "Pedro!"

"Lousy shot, kid," Edge growled. "A hundred miles is too far. Your old man just died."

Fury was gone in an instant from the handsome young face, and replaced by anguish as his dark eyes shifted their glassy stare from the smoking revolver to the dead man and back again.

"Madre de Dios!" he cried. And tears of despair erupted and coursed across his quivering cheeks.

He whirled as his sister once more shrieked his name. Closer now. Then Pedro lunged into a blind run for the door, his pumping legs kicking aside the chairs in his path.

"Sir, I am skilled in the ancient Oriental art of curing the sick by means of acupuncture!" the oddly attired man at the open door to the room section called.

Edge picked up the glass of whiskey and nodded towards the door as Pedro wrenched it open and raced outside.

"If you're ready to take a chance you might give the kid the needle, feller," the half-breed invited.

57

The man was confused and hesitant for a moment. Then he lowered his arms and picked up the skirts of his gown before giving chase to Pedro.

"Amor mio hermano!" Isabella cried in strident relief.

Edge ambled across the saloon, and halted on the threshold to swallow the rye in one gulp. He banged down the empty glass on a nearby table, then delved into a pocket of his pants, pulled out a handful of loose change and funnelled it into the glass.

"For the beer and liquor," he told the waxen-faced Fred, who was only now beginning to climb unsteadily to his feet. The man's shock expanded as he saw a sardonic grin spread across the bristled face. "The kid was supposed to pay, but seems he's in too much of a hurry to stand around."

Chapter Five

"STOP them!" the only able-bodied man left in the saloon shrieked. "They killed Barney Conners and Doc Vincent! Stop them murdering bastards!"

Pedro Montez was hurrying his sister toward the stalled wagon. The Oriental was hard on their heels, gaining on them despite the handicap of his long and capacious gown.

There was one other man on the broad street as Edge unhitched the reins of the mare from around the rail and swung up into the saddle. A rotund, bald-headed man in an apron appeared on the threshold of the City General Store. The lamplight against which he was silhouetted seemed much brighter than before. Just as the squares and wedges of yellow marking the windows and now open doors of the houses spread out from either side of the street appeared more intense, the effect caused by the advance of evening towards full night now that the sun was set. Between the widely spaced buildings flanking the street, shadowy figures could be seen running. The questions the townspeople yelled were merged into a confused din that made all but one indistinct.

"What the hell's happenin'?" the storekeeper demanded.

"Mexicans killing Americans!" Fred bellowed from the doorway of the saloon.

Pedro and Isabella Montez climbed up onto the seat of the wagon as the Oriental clambered over the tailgate. People from the houses burst out onto the street as the ox team was whipped into movement and Edge backed the mare away from the hitching rail.

"Race trouble!" the half-breed muttered through clenched teeth, wrenching on the reins to turn his mount, then thudding in his heels to demand a gallop in the wake of the wagon. "And seems like the minority are winning."

A short-lived volley of gunshots exploded bullets along the street. But it was small arms fire, triggered by men who, like the bartender of the Dragonara Hotel, were unwilling to shoot to kill unless there was a good reason. And no man with a gun in his hand could discern from the bedlam of shouting and shrieking voices, just why the wagon and horseman were making such a hurried retreat from Amity Falls. So the shots were fired out of excitement or for effect. And the escapers reached the safety of the trail across the western slope without being hit.

Edge slowed the mare to remain behind the bucking, rolling wagon, lips compressed and eyes cracked against the dust from under hooves and wheels, until they were beyond the ridge and out of sight of the town. He saw no sign that a posse was to be formed. He did see, vaguely in the darkness of the covered Studebaker, Senalda Montez and the new passenger flailing their arms at each other.

Then he swung to the side, passed the speeding wagon and glimpsed the rigid form of Pedro crouched on the seat, the girl clinging desperately to her brother as the wagon bucked beneath them.

He made no sign to them. Nor looked back over his shoulder. But, from the sounds of the frantic retreat assaulting his ears, he knew Pedro had turned the team to follow when he veered the mare on to a south heading fork of the trail beyond the ridge.

And the boy continued to take his cue from the half-breed, curtailing his snarling entreaties to the oxen and setting aside the whip as Edge reduced the speed of the mare. They were about a mile southwest of Amity Falls then, moving at a walking pace under the hard, bright light of a three-quarters moon. The chill of evening dried the sweat of exertion on every face as the rider adjusted the step of his mount to fall back alongside the front of the wagon.

Senalda Montez was venting a stream of harsh-toned Spanish and the Oriental was yelling back at her in his own tongue.

"So it's true about Mexicans and Chinese hating each other's guts," Edge said with a sigh.

Isabella snapped at her mother to be quiet and the woman's voice subsided to a low, ill-tempered muttering.

"Sir, in this instance you are only half right," the Oriental announced, thrusting his head out from the canvas flaps between the two Montez youngsters.

"Maybe because I'm only half Mexican, feller," Edge answered absently, glancing back and failing to see any sign of pursuit.

"For I am not Chinese. My name is Ree Maung. Mr. Ree. And I am from country of Siam, town of Chiengmai. Poet, philosopher and man of peace. Mostly poet."

"Not a doctor in there any place?" Edge wanted to know.

Isabella and Pedro had been as resentful of the passenger as their mother, but too breathless to voice their complaints. Abruptly, their mood changed.

"He says Antonio can be saved by pushing needles into him!" Senalda moaned.

Mr. Ree may have been any age from mid-twenties to late forties. He had that kind of face. Round and smooth skinned. His complexion was sallow and he was clean shaven—perhaps he never had to shave, like an Indian. It was a pleasant face with almond-shaped eyes that expressed gentleness no matter which other mood the rest of his features showed. His build was short, almost squat. He looked well fed. He was totally bald.

Pedro snorted and Isabella scowled.

"I've heard tell it works in China," Edge said evenly.

Mr. Ree nodded vigorously. "I have traveled widely in Asia, sir. Learned many things. Wherever I travel, I learn." His mouth suddenly looked sad. "But so many skills require implements, sir. It was necessary for me to leave Amity Falls in great haste. No time for me to gather my belongings."

Edge sighed. "You left your little black bag behind, uh?"

Mr. Ree shook his head, but remained sad. "Big red bag, sir."

"But you brought what you know and you've got your feet, feller," the half-breed pointed out, checking the moonlight bathed terrain spread out behind the wagon again.

"Sir?" Ree posed, perplexed.

"Do what you can for him. And it better be more than anyone else. Or you get to use your feet. A poet, philosopher, and man of peace is just so much excess baggage."

62

The little man from Siam showed anxiety now. Then he nodded and withdrew into the wagon.

"What happened, Pedro?" Isabella demanded.

The boy was staring ahead. After a brief experience of anger when he learned Ree was of little use to them, he had withdrawn into a private world of misery. If his sister's words penetrated it, he chose to pretend they did not. The girl swung her head to look pleadingly at Edge.

"The kid shot an unarmed man in the back," the half-breed supplied evenly, digging out the makings. "Back of the neck."

Isabella snapped her head around to stare in horror at Pedro. The boy remained rigid, moving only with the motion of the wagon.

"Lost his temper and your pa a doctor," Edge went on, rolling the cigarette.

Isabella's head moved from side to side, transferring her gaze from Pedro to Edge and back again. The horror stayed etched deep into her lovely face. "You did not prevent this?" she gasped into the silence as Edge struck a match on the side of the wagon seat and lit his cigarette.

"He was busy," Pedro supplied dully, announcing his awareness of the conversation. He raised a hand from the reins to trail a finger across his left cheek to the corner of his mouth. "Cutting a man's face, clean through. From here to here."

"*Madre de Dios!*" Isabella groaned.

"Ain't complaining about you blasting him, kid," Edge said. "Figured to do something about him myself, on account of that greaser talk. But your timing was way off."

Pedro nodded, his handsome young face still a mask of anguished remorse. "I understand, *hombre*. You had your drink before you used your razor against the man who served you."

"So that is how you justify *your* presence with us, *señor?*" Isabella snapped. "To teach evil to my brother by example?"

Edge shook his head. "You folks are heading in the same direction as I am, lady." His narrowed eyes beneath their hooded lids seemed to glint more brightly in the moonlight than they had in the sun as he made another overtly carnal survey of the girl's body. "So I'm just along for the ride."

The obvious meaning of his look and words did not embarrass her this time. They merely caused her disgust to deepen.

"You are an example of the kind of man I loathe and despise, *señor!*" she rasped through clenched teeth, wrenching her head around to stare along the trail as intently as her brother.

Edge arced his cigarette away into the night and maintained his concentration on the profile of Isabella's hard set face and rigid body for a moment longer.

"And you're an example of a fine woman." he muttered softly, heeling the mare into a canter. "Which is the only example I'm really interested in making."

Behind him, he heard Pedro urge greater speed from the ox team. But Isabella spoke sharply to him and the boy complied with her order. Edge rode no faster than an easy canter along a trail that rose and dipped, curved and switch-backed on the barren rockiness of the Continental Divide.

The lumbering wagon was long out of sight and earshot of the town when he veered off the trail to the right, following the course of a shallow stream into a broad canyon. There was grass in the canyon, and scattered stands of spruce. The stream was slow running, but its water was sweet. He checked that there was a steep, but negotiable exit from the far end of the canyon. Then he hobbled the mare and climbed up to the northern rim. From the highest point on the canyon wall he could see the moon-lighted landscape in sharp clarity over a distance of many miles.

He ignored the slow moving wagon for he had known it would be there. No other sign of life could be seen. Intervening ridges and rock outcrops caused many blind spots, but the half-breed was as satisfied as he could be with the canyon as a night camp when he climbed down again to the floor.

His horse was unsaddled and he had a pot of coffee bubbling on a small fire when the wagon came to a halt in the moon shadow of a rock overhang where he had established the camp. Isabella, tight-lipped and sullen, had the reins. Ree, looking around with keen interest, was beside her.

"Having a change of heart?" Edge posed with mild irony, lifting the pot from the flames and pouring coffee into a mug.

He was seated on his saddle, the Winchester out of the boot and resting against his thigh.

"I followed the tracks of your horse, *señor*," the girl admitted, not looking at him. "A man like you would know where it is best and safe to camp for the night."

"The enemies of the night/They are darker than those of day/So put aside your differences/Those with common cause/In the night," the little Siamese intoned, rather than spoke the words. Then he grinned and jumped to the ground with graceful agility. "A poem I have composed for this occasion. All my poetry is in the form of blank verse."

"Now is not the time for poetry, *señor!*" Isabella berated. "Deeds are required. Words are useless."

Ree executed a formal bow, a chastened expression on his round, smooth face. The gesture appeared perfectly natural to him, with no hint of patronization in his manner. "Of course, madam. I am yours to command."

He unhitched the oxen while Pedro attended to the saddle horse. Without asking permission, Isabella boiled up a pan of water and gave it to Ree, who took it into the wagon. Lamplight glowed behind the canvas. Pedro gathered fresh kindling for the fire and his sister prepared and cooked a meal of beef stew.

There was little talk, except in low tones between Senalda Montez and Ree, until Isabella acknowledged one debt to Edge by thrusting a plate of stew at him.

"Obliged," the half-breed responded.

Pedro, looking even younger in his misery, sat on a rock and ate the food with the actions of an automaton.

"And we would be once more grateful to you, *señor*," Isabella replied, squatting on her haunches beside the wheel to which Edge had once been tied, "if you will look at my father's injury. You have seen many men with bad wounds, I am sure."

"Enough," the half-breed answered, and eyed the girl with an expression as close as he could get to sympathy, "to know that a bullet in the belly is the worst kind. Short of a killing shot, if there's a doctor who knows his trade around. It's been inside him close to ten hours now. And he ain't woke up at all?"

"Not even for a moment. His breathing is bad and the wound—it smells."

"So me looking at it won't help, Isabella. Same as splashing water on it won't help."

"So there is nothing we can do, *señor*?" She put

down her plate, the food untouched, and crossed herself. "Except pray."

"That could help the way you feel," Edge allowed, spooning a final mouthful of stew into his mouth and standing up, hoisting the rifle. "And if you figure the prayer'll be heard, make it that your pa dies before he wakes up. Give you grief, but save him a lot of pain."

A sudden anxiety held back her threatened tears as she watched him take a calf-length black coat from his bedroll and shrug into it. "You are really going to leave us?"

"Be back," he answered. "And if you douse the fire maybe I'll find you all still alive. Keep warm with blankets."

Before he had reached the mouth of the canyon the flames of the campfire had been smothered with dirt. He turned left and made fast time back tracking along the trail. His expelled breath turned to gray vapor in the cold air of night. But the unaccustomed exercise of brisk walking kept him warm.

The small box canyon he had checked out when passing earlier was about a mile back towards Amity Falls. When he reached it, he spent about five minutes obliterating old signs and creating new, using his feet and the stock of the rifle to make it appear the wagon had turned off the trail and into the canyon. To a cautious tracker, the ruse would be obvious. But next, Edge went into the canyon to build and light a large fire, counting on pursuers to see the blaze and pay only scant attention to the disturbed dust at the entrance.

From the rim of this canyon his view of the surrounding country was more restricted than at the other. Except to the northwest, where he could see long stretches of the trail almost all the way back to the hill beyond which Amity Falls was sited.

Sitting down on a rock, hands thrust deep into his pockets and Winchester resting across his thighs, he began to feel the full discomfort of the moon-bright night. But he endured it without futile complaint and his mind was free of equally useless wishful thoughts of being close to the fire which created a tantalizingly warm glow within the canyon.

He had made his decision and put a plan of action to the test. And, as always, accepted the consequences with a stoic resolve. Perhaps he was wasting time and effort. Perhaps there would be no posse riding out from the grim and spartan town. Perhaps the claim of Isabella Montez that she despised him had not been merely a vocal outlet of anger to be regretted later.

Only time would tell. And the man called Edge was rich in time.

Fate had ordained that he should meet the girl. And the same fate had elected that he should feel about her in a way he had never felt about a woman before, not even Beth Day. Beth had happened over a period. With Isabella, it was immediate.

Because of the harshness of his experience, which had brutally fashioned the kind of man he was, it was impossible for him to express himself to her, or look at her, in the manner such a young and impressionable girl would expect. Maybe welcome. For she doubtless had romantic notions about love. And there was no romance in the soul of Edge: although his feeling for her went far deeper than the brand of animal lust which was all he was able to show.

Perhaps love. But he would never acknowledge it as such, even in his own mind. For everything and everybody he had ever loved had been cruelly taken from him.

Far off across the cold and barren mountain ridges,

68

a coyote howled. It sounded like the obscene laughter of a wicked destiny, relishing a preconceived triumph over an adversary doomed to lose.

And the six riders showed on the trail, galloping their horses around a curve at the center of a cloud of dust.

Edge was in cover, not silhouetted against the sky or the fire's glow. He did not move. He thought he knew why the sheriff of Amity Falls had delayed the departure of the posse. The lawman resisted impulsive action to avenge the death and injury of two of his fellow citizens. He knew those who had brought violence to his town were traveling by wagon, and probably that their progress was hampered further by the burden of a sick man. So he had elected to bide his time, to give his quarry a false sense of security, before setting out on an easy to follow track. And hit them when they were resting, thinking they were free and clear.

The posse was by turns in sight on the open trail or hidden by dips of rocky outcrops. Then, when the men comprising it saw the glow of the fire, the pace was slowed. A halt was called and conversation was exchanged. Moments later, the advance began again. Slowly, still on horseback. A quarter of a mile off, the men dismounted, tethered their animals to a thicket of brush, and covered the final stretch on foot.

Only then did the half-breed allow himself a tight, brief smile. He dropped forward onto his hands and knees and crawled away from the canyon rim.

The fire was low now, just as one would be after being left for several hours by people asleep. The posse from Amity Falls approached its light with cautious slowness. Edge was just as wary about making a noise, but he moved faster, having to cover a greater distance as he reached the same level as the men but swung wide of them.

Only the howls of the coyote, sounding intermittently and at a greater distance each time, marred the mountain silence. Until the tethered horses whinnied at the approach of a stranger. And Edge spoke softly to them, calming them in the gentle manner of a man who understood their nervousness.

The beat of the slow-moving hooves sounded loud to the ears of the half-breed as he unhitched the six geldings and led them away. But there were no shouts of alarm from the direction of the box canyon.

In a hollow two hundred feet off the trail, he used the razor from the neck pouch to cut through the cinch leather of each saddle so that a slight push tipped it to the ground. Next he cut the bridles and reins from the horses and headed all of them back toward Amity Falls before slapping two on the rump.

They lunged into motion with an explosion of clattering hooves against rock and hard-packed dirt.

Edge broke into a run at the same moment, away from the bolting horses and at an angle, back tracking on his route from the canyon rim.

He heard shouts above the diminishing beat of galloping hooves. And curled back his teeth to show another private smile. Until gunshots exploded.

Instinctively, he pumped the lever action of the Winchester and stooped into a half crouch. But no bullets cracked close to him. He straightened and started up the slope towards the canyon rim, constantly altering direction to put areas of cover close at hand should he need them. But the continuous barrage of rifle and small arms fire, competing with shouts of terror and screams of pain, was confined between the canyon walls.

70

Close to the top of the slope, he slowed, dropped out full length and bellied himself over the final ten feet.

The fire he had lit was now a heap of red embers. But the glow it emanated was enough to supplement the moonlight and illuminate almost the entire canyon floor.

Three figures were sprawled in the open, their clothes stained dark with fresh blood. Two were white men, shot in the back and transfixed by death close to the dying fire. One was a Shoshone brave, a bullet blasted into his heart, folded double against the dirt at the canyon entrance.

The other four men from Amity Falls were trapped at the blind end of the canyon. Their backs were to a sheer, thirty feet high wall of rock. Between them and a dozen or so Indians who had surprised them, the only cover was the scattering of boulders at the canyon entrance. The braves were in the secure cover of these rocks, firing at a measured pace towards the whites.

A third member of the posse was hit as Edge gained his vantage point. The man took the bullet in his throat and slid down the wall, leaving a slick trail of blood against the moon-bright rock. His death triggered fresh screams of terror from the survivors and sparked an even more frenetic fusillade of panicked shooting.

A careless brave was wounded in the shoulder and his shrieks of pain rose more shrilly than the groans of another brave with a shattered kneecap.

Edge was a dispassionate observer, witnessing the dying and the agony through narrowed eyes, the set of his thin lips betraying nothing of his thought processes. He had wanted only to delay the posse, possibly cause them to lose heart in the chase.

Two more white men died within two seconds of

each other. Both were hit in the chest, the impact of the killing bullets slamming them against the rock wall. Their corpses were rigid as they bounced, then became limp as they crumpled to the ground.

The half-breed had not known a band of hostile Shoshones would happen by at the right moment to box the posse in the blind canyon. But that was what had occurred. And the slaughter taking place below was of concern to him only in respect that any possible threat from the posse was now completely removed.

"Okay!" the last white man left alive shrieked. He hurled his rifle far ahead of him and thrust his arms high in the air. "Don't shoot no more! I'm finished."

The leader of the braves barked an order and all firing ceased. Gunsmoke, thicker and more acrid smelling than woodsmoke, eddied up out of the canyon. But it was not odor which caused Edge to grimace as the Indians rose from among the rocks and advanced along the canyon. Nor self-reproach for being responsible for what had happened, and what was happening, below him.

"On you, they ain't even started yet, feller," he growled softly.

The Shoshones were in the same sorry physical state as the ones who had attacked the crippled wagon. Ill-dressed, underfed and showing pocked and scabbed signs of disease. There was no elation in their victory. They approached the man from Amity Falls at a slow, weary pace. And their silence and complete lack of expression caused the white man's terror to expand.

Two braves halted and crouched down beside the dead at a midway point along the canyon. They began to strip the corpses of clothing, the Indian as well as the white men.

"Please!" the surviving member of the posse begged,

dropping to his knees. The impact jarred his entire body but he seemed to feel no pain. He extended his arms in front of him, still stiff, as the advancing Indians veered around the fire. "We didn't mean no harm to you! Honest we didn't! We was out hunting white men killers! We're a deputized posse! Take anythin' you want from me! But please, don't kill me!"

He was ignored by all but one of the Shoshones. As the other braves systematically robbed the dead of clothing and guns, the leader of the band halted in front of the pleading white man.

"I've got a wife and baby son! Another baby'll be here in three weeks! Please, Indian! Spare my life. For their sakes."

The man screamed as the muzzle of the Indian's Spencer came close to his face. The rifle was jerked upwards and the man's hat was knocked off his head. Out of moon shadow, his face was young, the naked fear it expressed starkly emphasised.

"I'll do anythin' you want!" he pleaded, his tone a croak now.

"Take off clothes, White Eyes."

"Sure! Sure!"

His shaking hands moved fast. Still on his knees, he stripped off his coat, vest, shirt and kerchief. Then unbuttoned the top of his long johns and wriggled out of it.

The braves were quicker in claiming the clothes of the dead. By the time the white man got to his feet and stooped to take off his boots, pants and long john underwear, every able-bodied Indian was watching him. One of them moved quickly forward to gather up the heap of discarded clothing.

Naked, the man looked younger still. His trembling flesh was dough white. He had little body hair. He

73

stood with his arms limp at his sides, making no attempt to cover his genitals.

"I done what you asked, Indian," he croaked.

The leader of the band turned just his head to look back along the canyon.

"One brave dead," he said. "Two wounded. That demands more than clothing, White Eyes."

The naked man raked his eyes around the impassive faces of the braves, then found they were trapped by the suddenly intense glare of the leader.

There was total silence and no movement for stretched seconds. Then the Shoshone leader whirled, snapping the Spencer repeater to his shoulder.

The brave with the shoulder wound was supporting the one with the shattered kneecap as they advanced slowly along the canyon floor. The rifle cracked twice in the hands of an expert marksman. The two wounded braves expressed fear but no resentment: Both were shot in the heart and they crumpled to the ground with their arms still locked together.

"We have little, White Eyes," their killer announced as he returned his attention to the naked prisoner. "Especially we do not have time or medicine to take care of injured braves. So, three dead."

The indifference of the Indians to the new killings witnessed that they had been prepared for the summary executions.

The prisoner fell to his knees again, venting a scream and clawing at the ground. The leader of the braves issued a curt order in his native tongue and stood aside as two braves stepped forward. Each stooped to grip a shoulder and wrist of the white man. Their touch silenced his vocal outlet of terror.

"It is because of the White Eyes that the Indian has so little!" the leader of the band said dully. "They have

74

robbed us for so long. Now it is our turn. We have died at their hand for so long. Now it is our turn."

He nodded and the two braves moved forward. The man trapped between them raised his head and looked towards the glowing embers of the fire immediately in front of him. His mouth gaped wide, but the prospect of what awaited him constricted his throat and no sound emerged. But there was no such restriction upon his bowels and bladder. An evil-smelling, liquid trail was left in the wake of his struggling form as he was hauled towards the fire.

Edge was no longer scowling. The man had acted stupidly and the half-breed had scant patience for those with such a failing. Trapped and out-numbered, the whites had been doomed to die from the moment the first shot of the battle was fired. The man now being dragged inexorably towards a humiliating and ag-onizing death could have chosen a quicker way, either by his own hand or in the process of fighting, perhaps taking some Shoshone braves with him.

He screamed now, as he felt the heat of the fire. The two braves raised him, so that just his knees, lower legs, and feet were on the ground. As they lowered him, he arched his back and bent his head towards the top of his spine.

The audience of Shoshones gathered around the fire. They gazed bleakly at the naked torso and the face of the man, red now in the reflected glow of the embers, beaded with sweat. Then the moisture evaporated as one of his captors placed a foot in the center of his back and eased him down.

The scream rose to an incredibly high pitch of shrillness, then was curtailed as his face was forced into the fire. A billow of black smoke rose. His hair caught fire and burned brightly for a moment. Sparks flew. His body spasmed once and was still. The braves released their hold on his arms. The aroma of roasted meat seemed to fill the entire world for a few seconds. Then the cold air of the mountain night neutralized it.

The depleted band of Indians moved towards the mouth of the canyon, clutching their battle booty of clothing and guns. The flesh of the new corpse was dough white again on his body and limbs. His head was charred black and featureless. Elsewhere on the canyon floor, the other naked dead grew colder in the night.

Edge eased up into a squat and remained where he was, until the hooves of unshod ponies beat at the ground. Then, as the sound diminished westwards, he rose and moved off. He returned to the night camp at an easy stroll.

Everyone there, with the exception of Antonio Montez, was fearfully awake. The wife of the critically injured man was in the rear of the wagon. The others were on the ground, draped with blankets.

"They sent out a posse from Amity Falls," Edge supplied evenly in response to the questioning looks directed at him through the silence.

"So much shooting, *hombre?*" Pedro rasped as the half-breed unfurled his bedroll. "You killed them all? Alone?"

"Ran off their horses is all," Edge replied, dragging his bedroll under the wagon and crawling into the meager shelter. "Figured to hold them up. Bunch of Shoshone braves stopped them. Dead."

Isabella gasped.

"Put it down to providence providing," the half-breed suggested, stretching out under his blankets and pushing his hat forward over his face. The Winchester was under the covers, too, his right hand curled around the frame.

"Pity those not who die/Who meant harm to you/For misfortune to such as they/Is salvation/To you."

"It is bad poetry, Isabella," Pedro said softly. "But the meaning of the Celestial's words makes good sense, I think."

Then there was silence, except for the low sounds of the Montez family and Ree bedding down for the night.

"Word was brought to Amity by the stage passengers yesterday," Ree announced after a few moments. "Many Indians have escaped from the Shoshone reservation in the west. Soldiers are trying to find them."

Nobody responded to the comment."

More silence.

"*Señor* Edge?"

"Yeah, lady?"

"Should not we stand guard? Perhaps the Indians will—"

"They're on the run from the army," the half-breed muttered. "They won't come back this way."

"Of course!" Ree put in, sounding relieved. "They will move far and fast to escape. You saw them doing this, sir?"

For a moment, Edge thought he could smell the cooking meat of the naked man's face on the glowing embers of the fire. Then he realized that it was the stench of Antonio's gangrenous wound that was assaulting his nostrils.

"Something like that, feller," he replied sleepily. "Guess you could say the last time I saw the Shoshones, they were forging ahead."

Chapter Six

EDGE slept as he always did. Shallowly, but soundly. His mind just below the level of awareness and his resting body an instant away from explosive response should danger threaten. Once, he came awake to sounds other than those made by the stirring horses and oxen. And raised his hat brim to look through the slits of his eyelids at the back of Pedro Montez. The boy, clutching his father's Sharps rifle, was heading towards the trail which crossed the mouth of the canyon.

Like an animal, Edge was aware of the youngster's return. He did not know how long the boy had been gone, but the sounds of his moving were familiar. And the half-breed slept on, resting his body and mind, restoring energies drained during the day, in the manner of a man well schooled in the arts of survival. The lessons of war now a habit.

He was first to wake as the light of dawn spread across the cloudless sky from the east. He lit a new fire on the ashes of the old, boiled a skillet of water and drank a mug of coffee as he shaved off the thick, black bristles, leaving only the drooping moustache at the top and corners of his mouth.

"You can be very handsome in the right circumstances, Edge," Isabella said, speaking for the first time

78

after watching him several moments. "For when I saw you yesterday, I thought you ugly. Yet, today—"

"You still look the same," he replied. "Good."

"Beauty is skin deep, they say," she responded grimly, tossing off her blankets and getting wearily to her feet. "I think there is much ugliness inside you. And I feel I am no better. In my heart, I can experience no pity for the men of that town who came after us."

She stretched, arching her back so that her tight-fitting shirt and pants emphasized even more the contours of her body and limbs.

Edge forced himself to look away from her. "I figure you'd feel real good to me, lady," he murmured.

"Father!" the girl blurted, ashamed she had forgotten. She whirled and hurried to the rear of the wagon.

"You continue to look at my sister in a way I do not like, *hombre*," Pedro growled as he folded up into a sitting posture, fisting the grit of sleep from his eyes.

"A woman to a man/Is a wondrous sight/And it must come to pass/That—"

"Shut your stupid mouth!" Pedro cut in on the newly awakened Ree. "And be on your way!"

Ree showed fear.

"You got any fancy words about a kid who likes looking at corpses, feller?" Edge asked evenly.

"My father lives still," Isabella announced as she climbed from the wagon. "But is much weaker."

"He is going to die!" Pedro snapped. "Until he does, we his family can take care of him. We can light our own fires and bathe his wound ourselves. We do not need you, or you!"

He shifted his scowling eyes between the Siamese and the half-breed.

"Pedro!" the girl snarled. "They have aided us.

They mean no harm to us. We will be the losers if they choose to leave."

Once more, the boy took heed of his sister's words. But his anger remained high, and he threw himself down onto his bedroll again, pulling the blanket over his head.

Isabella busied herself preparing and cooking breakfast. Edge fed the horses and oxen from supplies taken out of the wagon. Senalda stared vacantly at her dying husband. Pedro feigned sleep, or perhaps slept. Ree talked in a monotone, apparently uncaring whether anyone listened to him.

"I am a useless man. For none will take account of my poetry. I wander half the world, to bring comfort and understanding with words. But I receive only abuse. I am mistreated. When I work, as a man must to live, I am—"

"What were you doing in Amity Falls, *señor?*" Isabella asked. Neither her tone nor expression suggested interest. Perhaps there was sympathy in her indifference.

"Amity was another place on the path I travel, madam," he replied, obviously appreciating her intrusion on his monologue. "The people mistreated me, because I was a foreigner who does not look, talk or dress as they do. I offer my labor when my poetry falls upon their deaf ears. I was made to work in hotel. Menial chores, but worthy of payment. For one month I work. There is no payment. Only abuse. I am grateful to be rescued by other foreigners hated by the people of the evil town."

They ate breakfast. Then Ree bathed Antonio's stomach wound and applied a fresh dressing. Pedro prepared to shave, but then decided against it. Perhaps because he caught sight of his reflection in the basin of

80

water and liked the look of hardness which the bristles gave his face.

When they set off, the boy rode horseback on one side of the wagon and Edge on the other. Ree and Isabella were on the wagon seat, the Siamese having control of the team.

They were back on the open trail again, since it offered the only southerly route through the mountains for a heavy wagon. Although they were already at altitude and constantly on an upgrade, the sun got hotter as it inched up the eastern dome of the sky.

"I will scout ahead," Pedro announced when they had traveled more than two miles without conversation. "You watch the rear, *hombre!*"

Isabella looked sharply and nervously at Edge for his response to the snapped order. She was in time to see the half-breed direct a stream of saliva into the dust. Then she sighed as her brother galloped ahead of the wagon. And a fleeting smile of something akin to pride turned up the corners of her full mouth.

"He rides like he is part of the horse, does he not?"

"Yeah, which part?" Edge growled.

"I am of an age with Pedro," the girl said absently. "But I make allowances for his youth. Can not you do this?"

"I ain't killed him, have I?"

Isabella looked anxiously at the half-breed again.

He showed a cold grin. "But I ain't his sister. So don't ask me to love him."

"Thank you."

"Maybe you'll get around to doing that later. One good turn deserves another."

The girl wrenched her gaze away from the trap of Edge's blatant stare and directed her attention to the trail ahead.

Ree spared a gentle smile for each of them.

"Between love and hate/There is a line/One gentle breath of breeze/For fortune or evil/Will cause a turn/In a direction/For good or ill."

"*Señor* Ree, you are a very bad poet," Isabella muttered.

The stocky Siamese gave a shrug of resignation. "Or perhaps it is the time that is bad for my poems, madam?"

She seemed not to hear him in her too intent concentration upon the curving trail stretched out ahead of the slow moving wagon. The Oriental face, wearing an expression of gentle sadness, swung towards Edge.

The half-breed spat again into the dust.

Ree sighed once more. "So you think as madam does." Then he smiled again. "For you, such agreement is a start."

Edge pursed his lips. "A coming together of minds ain't what interests me, feller."

The girl snorted, much as her brother was prone to do. Then there was a new silence, until the wagon had covered the curve in the trail and was rolling through a pass.

"Pedro?" Isabella called suddenly.

The boy, still astride his horse, was halted at the other end of the pass, which was a narrow cleft between towering pinnacles. He beckoned with an arm gesture but did not turn around. Edge heeled the black mare into an easy canter, pulling ahead of the wagon.

"Men," the youngster announced as the half-breed stopped beside him. "A dozen or perhaps more. Not Indians. Beyond the mesa, *hombre*."

The terrain fell gently away to the south of the pass, into a broad and shallow valley that extended far to the south, until an east-west line of ridges blocked it. The intervening ground was featured with countless mesas and steep-sided bluffs, isolated hulks of rock and arm-like promontories which reached out from the valley sides. The trail twisted and turned between these obstacles. Stands of spruce shrouded the slopes. On the valley floor the soil looked sandy and supported only mesquite, greasewood and cactus. Nothing moved down there, in the harsh sunlight and deep, west-pointing shadows, until two horsemen showed on the trail where it snaked into view at the side of a red rock mesa. A mile and a half from where Ree halted the wagon behind Edge and Pedro in the pass.

"Soldiers!" the boy croaked, and jutted out his lower lip to send a stream of cool air up over his sweat-beaded face. "We have nothing to fear from them, eh, *hombre?*"

"I'm getting to think you're afraid of your own shadow, kid," Edge answered, counting fourteen blue-uniformed riders down in the valley riding double file.

"*Hombre*, we have reason——"

"They are hunting the renegade Indians, no doubt!" Isabella said quickly. "On such a mission, soldiers would carry medicine, I think."

"Among that many troopers, good and bad, lady," Edge supplied, blinking as sunlight glinted on the lenses of a pair of field glasses which were trained on the pass by one of the men heading up the column.

He heeled the mare into a walk down the slope. Pedro moved up alongside him and Ree set the wagon rolling behind.

"I have never had any reason to distrust the army of the United States, *hombre*," Pedro said, less easy in his mind than he had been before.

"You handle a rope good, kid," Edge told him.

83

"And throw a knife real well. You can handle a horse. Maybe you'll get better with a gun."

"You talk in riddles, *hombre.*"

"Matter of what you get used to. Your pa never let you fool with guns, uh?"

The boy snorted, then seemed to be ashamed of the thought which caused the sound. "We came north from San Parral to make money, *hombre.* Not spend it. Bullets cost money."

"And save lives, kid. If you know how to shoot them straight."

Pedro spat now. "I learn fast. I shot that Indian, too."

Edge nodded. "Sure you did. Now learn something about the army. On account you ain't never had reason to distrust it."

He and the boy, with the wagon close behind, had reached the foot of the slope. The patrol of troopers had been out of sight behind a bluff. Now they rode into sight again, in the same formation and at the same easy pace. Still too far off to be seen in detail. But the man with the field glasses continued to use them on the approaching civilians.

"You trust nobody, *señor,*" Isabella said flatly.

"Which gives us something else in common," the half-breed countered, and turned to show her a flinty grin.

"But the army is the protector of the people!" Pedro snapped.

"The army is made up of men, kid. All kinds. Good and bad and them that swing from one side to the other. Uncle Sam don't issue no halo along with a uniform."

"Distrust of all men is a burdensome traveling companion," Ree intoned.

"It's real light, feller," Edge answered, reining his mare to a halt. "And keeps me from being a dead weight."

The Siamese stopped the ox team. Pedro had ridden on, peering intently at the patrol. When he realized he was moving on alone, he snorted, jerked on the reins and backed the gelding to a position alongside the half-breed again.

The soldiers closed the gap on the halted horsemen and wagon. A lieutenant of about forty was in command, riding next to a sergeant ten years his senior. Both men were overweight and unfit. Behind them were a dozen enlisted men spanning an age range from about eighteen to close to sixty. They were as weary, sweaty, dirty, unshaven and disheveled as the officer and noncom.

It had obviously been a long, hard, exhausting patrol with little or nothing to relieve the monotony and frustration. Until the red-rimmed eyes of some of the men saw the near-beautiful face and full-figured body of Isabella Montez; then the attention of the less observant troopers was noisily directed towards her.

"Keep your stinkin' mouths shut!" the sergeant snarled, silencing the murmur of talk from the column as he surveyed the girl with as much keen, masculine interest as the troopers.

The green hills of Ireland could be heard in his voice. But he had last seen them a long and harsh time ago. He had a round, ugly, ruddy face with tiny eyes, a disjointed nose and heavy cheeks that sagged and pushed his mouth into a pout. He raised an arm to halt the column, the head of which was ten feet in front of Edge and Pedro.

"Good morning," the officer greeted, his voice an unfriendly growl. He did not touch the peak of his uniform cap. His face was cut on square lines. He had dull gray eyes, iron gray hair and a bushy moustache that was black. He had either gained a lot of weight since his uniform was issued, or he had drawn one that was two sizes too small. For the tarnished buttons of his tunic were put under great strain every time he took a breath. "Lieutenant Shotter commanding a patrol from Fort King. Tracking redskin renegades that busted out from the Lincoln Reservation. You people seen any redskins on your travels?"

He gave the same jaundiced look to Isabella as to the rest of the civilians.

Pedro nodded enthusiastically. "*Sí*, Lieutenant. Last night, south of the town of Amity Falls. And yesterday, in the morning. They attacked us then. Shoot my father. But we killed————."

"My father is very sick," Isabella interrupted. "He has a bad wound. Do you have a doctor with you? Or medicines, perhaps?"

She was uncomfortably aware of the lustful interest she was attracting from the troopers, and kept her anxious eyes fixed on the soured face of the officer. The news that he was at least a full night behind his quarry did not please Shotter.

"Many redskins?"

"Not so many now," Edge supplied.

"*Sí*, we killed four, in the morning of yesterday. Last night, the *hombre* here says that others were————."

"Please, my father!" Isabella insisted.

Senalda pushed her head out through the canvas flaps. The first glance at a second woman created more murmuring among the troopers. But the sergeant did not need to yell at the men this time. For a longer look at the aged, haggard and anxiety-riddled face of the girl's mother quelled the excitement.

"Where was he hit?" Shotter growled.

"In the gut and the bullet's still buried," Edge said.

"Since yesterday morning?" The officer grimaced. "I'm just a cavalry lieutenant, ma'am. Miracles have to come from a higher authority. Sergeant O'Keefe, move out the troop."

"Least we can take a look at the little lady's old man, Lieutenant!" one of the back markers of the column called. "Might be somethin' in our little old bag of medical tricks that'll help!"

He was tall and skinny. About forty, with sunken eyes that smiled easily, hollow cheeks and a deeply grooved chin. His tunic sleeves still carried the marks of when he had been stripped of his sergeant's chevrons.

"I ain't warnin' you no more times, Sheldon!" O'Keefe snarled. "You're on the fort commander's report for sure."

"That ain't nothin' new for Dan, sarge!" the man beside Sheldon taunted. "Nor me. And I reckon we should help these people."

There were nods and more vocal sounds of agreement with the two back markers. Apparently disinterested in the scene, Edge watched the soldiers carefully and saw that none allowed his attention to wander away from Isabella for more than a moment.

"You'll obey orders, damnit!" the non-com roared, his color turning a deeper shade of crimson as his anger rose.

Lieutenant Shotter revealed fear for an instant, then masked it behind a false front of weary resignation. "All right, sergeant!" he cut in, and silenced the troopers' noisy responses to O'Keefe's bluster. "We'll take a look at the injured man."

He transmitted a tacit message to the noncom, then gestured that they should both dismount.

"Stay in your saddles and behave respectful!" the sergeant ordered, then turned to follow Shotter to the rear of the wagon.

Senalda Montez smiled for the first time since Edge had met her. Then the troopers showed a mixture of grins and leers, with a great deal of lip-licking, when Isabella turned on the wagon seat and climbed through the flaps, presenting the trail-weary men with an uninterrupted view of her buttocks and thighs in the tight-fitting pants.

"Man, the end's in sight!" a grizzled veteran rasped.

"Don't it look good!" the youngest trooper muttered, pursing his lips to vent a low whistle.

"From every angle," another agreed.

"More curves than angles, seems to me," the emaciated Dan Sheldon growled.

The girl was hidden now, under the canvas top of the wagon. Ree was alone on the seat, smiling gently and foolishly, obviously afraid. Pedro Montez looked nervously from the Oriental to the excited soldiers to the impassive Edge.

"*Hombre*," he whispered. "There could be trouble, I think."

"Ain't what you're thinking that bothers me, kid," the half-breed muttered.

Despite the fact that Sheldon was no longer a sergeant, he still had a degree of authority over the other troopers. They all looked towards him, and did not dismount until he swung out of the saddle. Each man left his Spencer rifle in the boot. But all carried a Colt in a buttoned-down holster.

"You folks headin' back home to old Mexico?" the thin man asked as he sauntered along the double row of horses, his eyes smiling merrily.

"Guy in the flat hat and dress ain't Mexican, Dan,"

88

the youngest trooper pointed out as Sheldon emerged at the front of the dismounted soldiers. "He's a Chink."

"I am Siamese, if you please," Ree corrected, folding his arms and hiding his hands in the capacious sleeves of his smock.

"All you slit-eyed cats from across the ocean look the same to me," the young trooper replied with an indifferent shrug.

Sheldon laughed. "What you're ridin' with, Mr. Siamese, sure has some tail. But it ain't no dog."

"A lady," Edge pointed out. "Who ain't no tramp."

"My sister!" Pedro snapped.

Isabella had held the attention of the men when she was in sight. Since she went into the wagon, they had been intrigued by Ree. Only now did they look closely at Pedro and Edge—and saw the Mexican as a callow and frightened youth, and the half-breed as a full-grown man with more than mere bluff behind his cool and calm facade.

Sheldon glanced over his shoulder, perhaps to renew his confidence with the sight of the other troopers. Then, "Your word, mister."

"But your look, feller."

"What's the harm in lookin'? You another brother?"

"Looks can kill, feller. And thinking can end up being bad for a man. So best you get your mind off relations with the lady."

Sheldon laughed again and moved closer, the men crowding him from behind. Edge sat easy astride the black mare, his brown-skinned hands draped over the saddle horn. Abruptly, the trooper's emaciated face expressed snarling hatred. His tone was a match.

"I have enough of friggin' officers tellin' me what to

do, mister! And I sure ain't takin' no orders from a stinkin' civilian!"

"Wasn't an order, feller," the half-breed replied evenly. "Just a suggestion."

The smile was back in the dark eyes of Sheldon. And the men, who had become nervously expectant when his anger flared, showed smiles of their own.

Pedro snorted.

"Well, I guess that's all right then," Sheldon allowed, ambling past the two mounted men, trailed by the others.

"Just one thing," Edge added, turning in the saddle to watch as the men gathered at the side of the wagon. "You don't follow it, I'll kill you."

His right hand had moved from the saddlehorn to drape the butt of his holstered Colt. In the moment of shocked silence, when every face was turned towards him, this slight alteration in his casual posture was seen by all.

There was more than mere nervousness among the troopers now. Deep-seated fear that they had not been mistaken in seeing something mean and evil behind the nonchalant shell of Edge. They looked towards Sheldon again, and he responded with a glower of contempt.

"That's easy for a man with a gun in his hand to say."

"And do, feller. You and your buddies want to mount up?"

"Sheldon!" O'Keefe yelled. "What's goin' on out there?"

The scowl on the hollow-cheeked face became a leer. His eyes stayed fixed upon the impassive face of Edge, but his sneering words were directed at the sergeant. "Like to know what's goin' on in there, Sarge! With you and the lieutenant and a couple of—"

Edge pulled both his feet clear of the stirrups. He lifted his left leg high, folding it and swinging it clear of the horse's neck as he turned and slid clear of the saddle. The Colt was drawn while he was in mid-air and leveled as he landed, perfectly balanced, on the ground, ready cocked.

"Holy—" the youngest trooper started.

The gun bucked in the half-breed's hand. Blue smoke wisped from the muzzle. The range was no more than ten feet and produced a freak hit as Sheldon turned away in terror, bobbing down at the same time. The bullet intended for his heart took him in the side of the neck, closer to the front than the rear. It bored a hole through flesh, tore into his windpipe, and ripped a tunnel through more flesh before bursting clear on the other side. And still had enough velocity to reach the side of the wagon seat and ricochet off metalwork to the ground.

Something glinted brightly in the strong morning sunlight. Just a tiny splash of color against drabness.

Many throats voiced shock. Sheldon's spilled blood tried to find a low point. But his dying breath forced it up and out. It gushed from beneath his arched upper lip in a crimson torrent to form a quickly fading stain on the arid ground. As if he was ashamed of the mess he had made, Sheldon dropped to his knees, then fell forward across the blood. The death rattle had a moist sound. Then he was silent and still.

"You fellers see how easy?" Edge asked evenly, sliding the Colt back into the holster but keeping his hand fisted around the butt.

"—cow!" the youngest trooper finished.

"What the—, sergeant!" Shotter roared.

91

O'Keefe lunged from the rear of the wagon, Colt drawn. The lieutenant was right behind him, but stumbled in his haste.

"Gold!" a trooper exclaimed shrilly. "Look! The damn wagon's made of friggin' gold!"

The men had scuttled away from the collapsing body of Sheldon. Now they surged closer, unconcerned that they were trampling on a corpse, to look at the area of metalwork where the bullet had ricocheted. Edge had just a moment to see again the glint of gold which had caught his eye at the instant of Sheldon's dying, where lead had scratched the paint to reveal what was beneath. Then the heads and shoulders of excited troopers blocked his view.

"Reach, all three of you guys!"

The trooper who gave the order had a knife scar on his forehead and one eye that opened wider than the other. He broke from the cluster of excited men with his Colt drawn and leveled at Edge.

"Do it, and no one gets hurt!" he snapped. "Don't, and Dan Sheldon has company."

"That's a feller I wouldn't want to be seen dead with," Edge said, pushing his arms above his head. Only the growl in his tone hinted at the degree of anger he felt. Self-anger at not being ready, gun drawn again, for the new move. For he had allowed his mind to wander into the past and fasten momentarily upon a memory that served no useful purpose. Of a time in the timberland of the northwest when he had used a similar ruse to disguise the precious freight of a wagon.

"*Madre de Dios!*" Pedro croaked, and reached for the old Griswold in his holster.

"You ready to go see her!" the youngest trooper, of an age with Pedro, growled.

He had come clear of the group now, gun out of the holster and angled up at the Mexican.

"In death, nothing is gained. All is lost." As he intoned this philosophy, Ree unfolded his arms and raised them.

Pedro's eyes, ablaze with anger and then dulling to helplessness, moved from the Siamese to Edge to the troopers. All the soldiers were unbuttoning their holster flaps and pulling out Colts. His shoulders sagged, then were forced up again as he clawed his hands into the air.

"What the friggin' hell is goin' on, you men?" O'Keefe demanded.

One of the troopers swung a gun to cover the sergeant. A second drew a bead on Lieutenant Shotter.

"Pedro? *Señor* Edge?" There was a note close to panic in the voice of Isabella.

"Shut up!" the scar-faced trooper shrieked. "Shut up, the stinkin' lot of you crud! And friggin' listen!"

Some of the troopers, with guns drawn but aimed at nothing or nobody, expressed as much confusion and shock as was evident on the faces of the officer and noncom.

Then the ringleader moderated his tone and filled the sudden silence with words that spread smiles of glee across the tired, unshaven, dirt-grimed faces. He continued to concentrate his gaze and the aim of his gun on Edge, but addressed everyone.

"I'm sick of this cruddin' army. And I figure I ain't alone in that. Not after a whole friggin' year of ridin' herd on a bunch of stinkin' Injuns. Not after ridin' ten lousy days across this stinkin' country in this cruddin' heat lookin' for some shit-head Injuns that took off. And I figure the gold on this cruddin' wagon is gonna

93

buy me a ticket outta the cruddin' army. Buy tickets out for all that want 'em."

"Holy cow, yeah!" the youngest trooper yelled in high excitement.

There were nods and shouts of agreement from the rest of the enlisted men, some more enthusiastic than others. But the minority prepared to go along with the majority.

"That's mutiny, Fontaine!" O'Keefe said thickly.

"And desertion!" Shotter augmented, on a spray of spittle.

Every trooper had a target for his revolver now. As they were persuaded by the curse-riddled words of Fontaine, each previously uncommitted man leveled his gun at Pedro, or Ree, or Edge, or the officer and noncom. Thus, as Fontaine turned, swinging his Colt away from the half-breed, the threat of death was still directed at Edge.

"Firin' squad crimes," the scar-faced man growled. "Just as soon hang. If I'm caught. For murder."

He shot O'Keefe first, because the pouting-lipped sergeant had a gun in his hand. A neat hole appeared in his chest, left of center. By the time he had taken a surprised step backwards and started to fall, there was an untidy stain around the puncture. And Lieutenant Shotter was a moment away from dying. His straining tunic was holed lower down. And much more blood from a damaged lung spewed from his mouth than blossomed around the external wound. Much as Sheldon had done, he dropped to his knees and tipped forward.

Only Senalda Montez screamed. But soft-spoken Mexican words from Isabella quieted the woman.

"The army might not be so bad, it wasn't for cruddin' officers and stinkin' noncoms," Fontaine muttered,

94

as he cocked the Colt, bringing it back to cover Edge. "Why I don't hold it against you for blastin' that bastard Sheldon. Before he got busted, he was a sergeant. Worst kind."

"I ain't in the market for no citations, feller," the half-breed said.

Fontaine showed a thin smile. "I ain't givin' 'em, mister. Ain't givin' nothin' to nobody. Just lettin' you people keep your lives. And that not for nothin'. Exchange is no robbery. We take the wagon, your guns, and your horses. Sound fair to you?"

"I ain't in no position to be objectionable, feller."

"What about the girl, Ned?" the youngest trooper said, licking his lips.

"*Señor*—" Pedro started angrily.

"Shut up!" Fontaine snarled, then eyed Edge pensively. When he narrowed his eyes, one was more closed than the other. "She your girl?"

"It's a long way to Mexico. And a matter of opinion. Hers."

A nod. "You did me a favor. All of us a favor. Blastin' that bastard Sheldon and showing us the gold at the same time. All the metal on the wagon gold?"

"I wouldn't know, feller. And that's a matter of fact."

He shifted his narrow-eyed gaze to Pedro. The boy compressed his lips and, despite the thick bristles on his face, looked like a sullen child.

"We can find out for ourselves," Fontaine pointed out. "But you won't be around to see us."

"All of it that does not carry excessive strain," Isabella called from inside the wagon.

"Thanks," Fontaine responded, and returned his attention to Edge. "That's a lot, mister. Enough to buy all of us lots of women. As well as a lot of friggin' other frills the cruddin' army never give us. So you get to keep the girl. Make a man like you less inclined to come after us, I reckon."

"And I reckon it'd be easier—and safer—to blast all three of them and take the women along."

This from the youngest trooper.

Edge eyed him long and hard for the first time. He was a blond, with regular features, blue eyes, and a complexion just recovering from acne. When his skin was clear, he would be handsome. He had a slender body and a prominent bulge at the crotch of his pants. Despite the gun in his hand, which he seemed about to swing away from Pedro towards the half-breed, the glittering eyes of Edge sparked fear inside him.

"Shut up, Hardy!" Fontaine rasped. "Deal's made and I don't break my word." He grinned around at the troopers. "Didn't I tell you guys that one day I'd figure a way outta the cruddin' army for us?"

"You sure enough did that!" the elderly veteran agreed. "Shall I get the guns off 'em, Bill?"

"Do that, Mason. Then tie 'em up. Women, too. And get the feller outta the wagon. I can smell the stink of him from here. And I figure life for us is gonna be sweet smelling from here on in."

"A rose in bloom/Has a perfume that is sweet/But it must fade and wither/And be dead/Its fragrance then/Like all things rotted."

"He calls it poetry," Edge supplied as several of the troopers glanced suspiciously at the intoning Oriental.

Ned Fontaine blinked. "He crazy, or somethin'?"

"Don't seem a lot of rhyme or reason to him," the half-breed allowed as Mason circled around him and pulled the Colt from his holster.

Other troopers began to help the veteran, disarming Pedro, urging the two women out of the wagon and lifting the unconscious Antonio to the ground. Then a coil of rope from the Montez wagon was cut into lengths and all the civilians except the wounded man were tied, hand and foot. They sat in a group at the side of the trail and would be many hundred yards from the nearest shade once the wagon had moved.

"The time of my father's dying is close," Isabella said forcefully as the troopers prepared to leave. Fontaine and Hardy were up on the wagon seat. The rest of the men were mounted. Spare horses were hitched to the wagon tailgate. "Perhaps you would do us a favor to kill us now. It will take us a long time to die in this wilderness."

The regret expressed by many of the red-rimmed eyes fastened on the girl had little to do with her words. For the attention was focused upon her body rather than her face.

"I reckon you can make it until tomorrow, honey," Fontaine answered. "Stage'll be by here then. Northbound. We ain't headin' north no more, though. *Adios, amigos.*"

He cracked the whip across the backs of the ox team and kicked off the brake lever.

"Hasta la vista," Edge growled against the sound of turning wheelrims and clopping hooves.

Dust rose and settled on the securely bound living, the raggedly breathing dying, and the inert dead.

Pedro spat. "All is lost, *hombre.* We will never see them or the wagon again."

Fontaine cracked the whip harder and yelled to demand more speed from the oxen.

"Creo que sí, mi hermano," Isabella agreed morosely.

"The situation is indeed very bad," Ree added with

97

gentle sadness. "It would have been better for me to remain in Amity Falls."

Senalda Montez remained silent, tilting herself over onto her side, resting her head close to that of her husband and spilling tears as she gazed at his profile.

"Ain't nothing lost until something's won," Edge said evenly.

The boy chose to snort this time. "We are falling farther behind with every moment that passes, *hombre!*"

"You have a plan in your mind, *señor?*" Isabella asked, gazing intently at the half-breed.

The interest of the Siamese was also aroused.

"Same goal as at the start," Edge told her. "Still figure to score."

Chapter Seven

"SEÑOR, you are no better than those lusting, evil creatures who robbed us and left us here!" Isabella snapped.

"Worse even, I think!" her brother snarled. "At least they give us a chance to live. You murdered a man without giving him the opportunity to draw against you. You have no code of honor, *hombre!*"

Edge continued to direct his narrow-eyed gaze along the trail. The wagon and riders were out of sight now, beyond the curved arm of a bluff. But they would come into view again and be lost several times before they were out of the valley. Thus, the troopers would have equal opportunities to look back and see the apparently helpless group of prisoners they had abandoned.

"*Sí!*" the girl exclaimed bitterly. "To have my reputation defended by such a cold-blooded act of killing does not impress me." She shook her head violently from side to side, agreeing with herself. The anger and confusion visible through her swinging black hair gave her face a new kind of beauty. "And those men—those soldiers. Would they have stood idly by while other white men were being massacred by Indians? As you did."

"You are a coward, *hombre!*" Pedro returned to the

attack with more venom than before in his tone. "What happened to your big talk of pointing guns when the soldiers were here? I did not hear any such warning!"

"I feel you malign Mr. Edge," Ree said gently when the half-breed failed to respond to the verbal assaults with a glance or even a slight alteration in the impassive set of his features. "Honor is a fine word to relish in security and safety. When deadly danger threatens, to consider an honorable solution is foolish in the extreme."

"If he feels thus, why did he consider my honor?" Isabella demanded, her anger unabated. "Well, *Señor* Edge?"

"That's about it, lady," the half-breed growled. "I'm fussy about whose dipper goes into it before mine."

Pedro was about to spit, but choked on the saliva. "*Hombre*, one of us will surely kill the other!" he croaked.

"As for the posse from Amity Falls," Ree went on, as calmly as before. "Would those men have assisted us if it were we who suffered an Indian attack? Perhaps. But only to hang us."

The girl spared a portion of her scowling disgust for the Siamese with the gentle eyes. "If you have so little regard for human life, you and Edge are two of a kind, *señor!*"

"Make that three while your pa stays alive, Isabella," Edge corrected, just a trace of a rasp in his voice. "Or maybe even six. Maybe that's why I let things be last night. Hadn't been for some of those Shoshones' buddies I'd be deader than—"

"It is a matter of degree!" the girl cut in. Her voice was harsh and her dark eyes gleamed with rage. But then her mood moderated as she turned her head to stare after the departing wagon, which was in sight again. "San Parral is a poor village in the barren land of the Sierra Madre. My father was blacksmith and mayor of the village. He is a fine man who feels deeply for the people in their poverty. We come to the United States. We do this not to escape but to seek wealth to bring back to the people of San Parral. Two other families do this with us. Men who, like my father, do not work in the arid fields and can be spared."

The wagon and riders, comprising a mere indistinct blur in the distance now, went from sight around a mesa. But the girl continued to stare in the same direction.

"For three years we scratched and clawed among the cold mountains of Montana. We found gold. In tiny amounts. But we stored it carefully, using little for our own daily needs."

Large tears ballooned at the corners of her eyes and ran fast down her cheeks.

"When Father said it was time to take what we had and return to San Parral, the other families would not leave. One man, Jose Lajous who owned the cantina at San Parral, attempted to steal our gold. My father was forced to kill him."

"It was a fair fight, *hombre!*" Pedro interjected.

Edge glanced at Antonio Montez, who no longer looked big and powerful. Just very old, very gray and very weak. "Every man gets lucky sometimes, kid," he muttered.

"My father knew the journey to our home village would be long and arduous," the girl went on, as if there had been no interruptions. "And that it would be even more dangerous if we carried the gold openly. So he forged it into shapes that could be painted and fitted to the wagon."

She sighed and her eyes, as they swung towards

101

Edge again, seemed to be transmitting a plea for understanding. "Those others from San Parral, who were seeking gold in Montana for selfish reasons, they saw this. And they had much hatred for us, because Jose Lajous had been killed. When you approached us, *señor*, looking much like a Mexican, looking much—" She shrugged. "We thought the worst. *Sí*, had you died then, your death would have been a dishonor for us. But our motive was to safeguard the gold. Not to keep for ourselves. But to bring hope to the villagers of San Parral. A matter of degree. We resort to violence with abhorrence but for a high ideal. You appear to relish it, killing merely for the sake of ingratiating yourself with me. In vain, *señor*. For I come only to despise you even more."

Now she stared down at her own feet, which were lashed securely together at the ankles.

Her mother struggled up into a sitting posture again and shook her head as she looked morosely at Edge. "I think not, Isabella," she said dully. "A man such as this, if he wanted a woman, he would take her. I think he wants something else. Perhaps he did not know what it was until the bullet revealed the gold."

"*Sí!*" Pedro exclaimed, emerging from a period of pensive detachment while his eyes had constantly raked the slumped corpses of the three soldiers. "I think that is right. You are—what is the American word—an opportunist. *Sí*." He snorted. "But it is useless for you to stare so intently towards the wagon, *hombre*. The gold it carries is as lost to you as to us."

The ancient Studebaker and its escort of deserting troopers could no longer be seen against the line of ridges blocking the southern end of the valley.

"You feel as bad about me as the others, feller?" Edge asked Ree.

"Judge not a man until/By deed or word he reveals/His nature—"

"Guess you're trying to tell me no, uh?" the half-breed interrupted.

"Does it matter, sir?" He glanced around him. "In the present circumstances?"

"Yeah, it's a matter of life or death. Mine. Whether you'll cut my throat or the ropes holding my wrists together."

Senalda Montez stared at Edge in bewilderment, which deepened as a broad grin spread across the gentle face of the Siamese.

"Your razor!" Ree exclaimed.

The older woman remained confused. But Pedro had seen Edge's attack on the bartender in Amity Falls. And Isabella had seen the half-breed return the razor to the pouch after shaving with it that morning.

"It's sharper than you folks," Edge muttered as the boy and the girl came close to smiling. "So go easy with it, feller."

"You need me, sir," the Siamese said, going over on to his side, then folding his knees and struggling upright. The exertion left him breathless. "But when we are free, we will all need you. For your resourcefulness."

He had to move in short, awkward jumps, then turn to put his back to the seated half-breed. He crouched, pushing his tied hands out behind him, fingers delving into Edge's black hair and probing over the shirt collar to grip the razor. He straightened to draw it from the neck pouch, then lowered himself to the ground again and began to saw at the ropes binding Edge's wrists.

"Easy, feller," the half-breed reminded, "or I could lose a lot of my resources through a main artery."

Ree muttered a word of apology in his own language

103

and slowed his frenetic action with the blade. But it took only moments for the razor to cut through the rope. Then Edge cut through the bonds at his ankles, freed Ree, and gave him the blade to attend to Senalda, Isabella, and Pedro.

He went to the body of Lieutenant Shotter, waved a hand at the flies massed on the congealed blood of the wound, and took the field glasses from around the neck of the corpse.

Through their lenses, the distant line of ridges leapt closer. Nothing could be seen moving among the low peaks.

"Sir," Ree said.

Edge lowered the field glasses and accepted the razor, pushing it back into the pouch.

The Siamese was inscrutably patient. Senalda was crouched beside her husband. Isabella and Pedro massaged their wrists and eyed their parents helplessly.

"The wagon is no longer to be seen, *hombre?*" Pedro said at length.

"They got my horse, gear, and guns, kid."

Isabella suddenly wrung her hands. "There has been enough talk of motives! But we can do nothing to achieve our aims while my father lives."

Senalda shrieked and threw herself across Antonio, as if fearful someone was about to speed his inevitable end.

Pedro draped an arm briefly across the shoulders of his sister, then stood apart from her. "We can carry him!" He pointed towards Ree. "You. We rescued you from Amity Falls and you have been useless to us until now. You will help me carry him."

"To move him will kill him!" Senalda moaned.

Isabella nodded. "*Sí, mi madre.* But if Father could speak, he would tell us to leave him. That to get the

104

gold to San Parral is the most important thing. More important than his life. He cannot speak. So we must do what we think is best."

"Celestial?" Pedro demanded, crossing to stoop at the head of his father as Isabella pulled her mother away.

"For as long as I can," Ree said, moving to take the ankles of Antonio.

"As long as it is necessary," Pedro corrected.

Through the furnace heat of morning, midday, and afternoon the group walked the length of the valley and up towards the ridges. There was no talk. Not even when Pedro Montez—at least half the age of Mr. Ree—staggered and fell, and Edge draped the heavy form of the senseless Antonio over his shoulders to spell both the other men for more than half a mile.

There was a water hole on the high ground and they rested there, on the sign left by the passing wagon and animals. Everyone knew there had been water closer at hand among the timber growing on both sides of the valley. But there had been a tacit agreement to stay on the trail of the quarry.

The respite was a short one, and as they prepared to move on again, Ree said,

"Would it not be better for the madams to stay here with the casualty? We could travel faster. And, should we meet with the soldiers, the madams, they will not be of—"

"No!" Pedro and Isabella replied in unison.

Ree looked at Edge for support.

"Guess *Señora* Montez agrees with them, feller," the half-breed said. "And with one silent partner in the company, we're outvoted."

The Siamese sighed wearily as he stooped to take hold of Antonio's ankles. "It was just a suggestion."

105

"They're really set against folks being suggestive," Edge muttered, moving out from under the shade of the trees around the water hole.

It was necessary to rest more often throughout the remainder of the hot afternoon and during the cool evening. Water was plentiful, but they had all been without food since the dawn breakfast. And the effects of the exhausting walk were cumulative.

When it was full night, the moon seeming to radiate intense cold in the same manner the sun had clamped blistering heat over the country, they reached a point where the tracks left by the wagon and horses led off the trail to the west. Into another valley, much longer, deeper, and with steeper sides than the one where they had met the army patrol.

Antonio Montez died there.

Whatever subconscious effort of will had caused him to cling on to life for so many grueling hours was abruptly extinguished. As the tall, lean half-breed lowered the Mexican gently to the hard ground, there was a soft sigh. The man's chest sank and did not rise again. His mouth fell open and his eyes remained closed. The stench emanating from beneath the crude and filthy dressing bandaged to his belly seemed much stronger for a moment. Then a cutting breeze wafted along the valley and masked the pungent odor.

"Antonio is dead," Senalda said dully, without stooping to look more closely. "Your father has gone to rest."

"It was to be," Pedro murmured.

Isabella made to place an arm around her mother's shoulders. But the woman shook her head.

"It is all right. I am cried dry of tears."

Ree drew in a deep breath. "When a life is closed/When the final—"

Edge reached out, gripped the brim of the Oriental's coolie hat, and wrenched it down over the gently melancholy face of the man. "They've got their own words for this, feller," he said, as the Montez family crossed themselves and sank to their knees.

Then he moved away, out of earshot of the murmured prayer and with his back to the group. Ree joined him, after setting his hat back squarely on his head. Edge rolled and lit a cigarette, gazing down the length of the valley.

"You think we have a chance to find the soldiers, sir?" Ree asked after a while.

"Better now we're traveling light, feller."

"He has been death, waiting to die, for a long time. A relief to everyone."

"What are you waiting for, feller?"

"I do not understand, sir."

"You were in Amity Falls a month. You know the stage schedules, I guess. Was Fontaine telling it straight about one coming north tomorrow?"

"Oh, yes. There is one every day, sir. From Leadville and Mountain City to Amity Falls and then on to Denver. A journey of many days, but mostly the stage is on time."

"So why didn't you wait for it, feller? Fontaine and his buddies didn't take anything that belonged to you."

"To go back to Amity Falls?" Ree exclaimed.

"You didn't kill anyone there. But you been working real hard to keep from going back."

"There is nothing more to say." It was Pedro Montez who called this, drawing the attention of Edge and Ree. He and his mother and sister were up off their knees, standing close together and gazing at the two men and beyond them along the valley.

"Just to do," Isabella added.

107

And the trio moved away from the body. The corpse was far enough off the trail and into the valley not to be visible to any passing stage passenger or horserider.

"The buzzards will take care of what is left of my father now that his soul has departed the shell," the girl explained to the shocked and puzzled Siamese. "Or the coyotes. He would not much care, if he knew it was not possible that he could be laid to rest beside the church in San Parral."

"And you care not at all, eh, *hombre?*" Pedro growled, stepping slightly ahead of his mother and sister in passing the stationary half-breed and Siamese. "What becomes of the dead is even less important than what happens to the living."

"Figure a funeral is a family affair, kid," Edge replied evenly, no hint of criticism in his tone as he crushed the cigarette out under his boot heel. "Always did bury my own dead."

When he moved off, the Montez group and Ree hurried to catch up with him.

"In troubled, but less brutal times, *señor*, we too behaved in a more civilized manner," Isabella said flatly, without turning her head. "But we have come to accept that we must act according to the standard set for us."

Edge spat at the ground ahead of him, and muttered, "In this case, the gold standard."

Chapter Eight

"THEY are stupid!" Pedro rasped between clenched teeth. "Very stupid to leave us alive and very stupid to waste time in sleep."

"Learn from other men's mistakes and you could live to be very old, kid," Edge answered softly.

"If he is to become as embittered and brutal as you by such lessons, I would prefer my son be dead before his next *cumpleaños*, Senalda Montez snapped but kept her voice low.

"Your daughter has a lot of faith in providence, *señora*," Edge muttered. "For your son's sake, best you don't tempt it."

They had found the stolen wagon and the deserters who had taken it—at the end of another grueling walk—the length of the valley, then southwards again across a wide plateau and around a lake which was the source of many streams.

Had they still been burdened by the dying Antonio, they could not have made it. Even without this difficulty, they were close to complete exhaustion as they sank to the ground and peered at their reward for the effort. Hunger was not so bad now. But every muscle in every body ached for prolonged rest. And the cold of the mountain air, compounded by the soakings they had received crossing fast-running icy streams, created a different kind of pain.

"You knew we would find them tonight, didn't you, señor?" Isabella asked.

They were on the southwestern shore of the moon-silvered lake, on the fringe of a stand of mixed spruce, cottonwood, and aspen. The wagon was parked in a glade two hundred feet away, the oxen and horses tethered to tree branches, the men under blankets on the ground. There had been a cooking fire, but it had been doused before the deserters bedded down.

Edge rechecked his count of eleven sleeping men and looked at the girl. She had fallen full-length into the last stream they crossed. Her hair was plastered tightly to her head and her shirt clung so closely to her upper body that it outlined the cold-distended nipples of her full breasts. She had to clench her teeth to keep them from rattling. But her eyes expressed something close to gratitude.

Without the half-breed, the Montez family and Mr. Ree would have been indulging their weariness with rest, far from the timber stand beside the lake. For the discomfort and physical pain of the long walk through the night had quickly drained the Mexicans of the determination sparked by the death of Antonio. And the Siamese had always been quick to agree when the suggestion that they should halt was voiced.

Edge had never argued—had merely continued to move at the same even pace, lips set in a firm line and cracked, glinting eyes fixed on the easy-to-follow sign of a heavy wagon and sixteen horses, nine of them with riders in the saddle.

"Figured there was a good chance," he answered, conscious of the effort it took, even in these circumstances, for him to hold his gaze on her face. "On account of while they keep the wagon in one piece, they can't travel much faster than folks on foot. Slower even, across this kind of country."

"And you knew, sir, they would not expect to be apprehended so soon," Ree whispered.

"As I said, very stupid," Pedro growled. "Eleven. The same number who stole our wagon. All asleep, like untroubled babies."

He spat into the lush grass that grew long and thick among the tree trunks.

Edge sighed. "You reckon you can hold back on the spitting and snorting for a while, kid?" he asked.

"You have a plan, *hombre?*"

"Nothing special. And ain't worth nothing if there's any noise before the right time."

The boy scowled. "In Montana, *hombre*, I once got within ten feet of a bull moose before he knew I was there. What do you want me to do?"

"Keep in mind that silence is golden. And stay this far away from these fellers until I get back."

Pedro got set to protest, but Isabella clamped a hand over his mouth. Ree sighed his relief that he had no part in the half-breed's plan, then expressed gentle nervousness when Senalda Montez asked:

"What if you do not come back, *señor?*"

Edge showed his teeth in a grin that drew nothing from his glittering eyes. "Dead men tell no tales, *señora*. And make no plans." He started to move off, then held back for a moment. "Maybe your boy could do some more spitting. Drown those fellers."

He went then. Quickly and silently, on a semi-circular course through the timber around the glade. And did not turn to move closer to the sleeping men until he was at the furtherest point from the tethered animals and nearest to the wagon. He remained upright

111

until he lost the cover and moon shadow of the trees, then went down on his hands and knees to crawl out into the glade and under the wagon.

The trampled grass was sopping wet with dew. But it was easy to disregard physical discomfort now. For he was within a few feet of eleven men, all of whom would kill him if he gave them the opportunity. All of them sleeping soundly, but with a rifle and revolver close by. The half-breed had only the razor in the neck pouch and the element of surprise.

So his life was on the line again. As it had been countless times since that first Indian attack on the Iowa farmstead long ago. But never before had he maneuvered himself into such a precarious position for such a vacuous—perhaps fatuous—reason. For the discovery of the wagon's secret had not changed his motivation in staying with the Montez family. He had no selfish designs on the gold and cared nothing for the Mexican peons of San Parral it intended to help. No, it was simply the need to satisfy his carnal lust for the body of a young woman—whose every curve drove him crazy with desire—which had triggered his responses since he first saw her.

Pausing for a moment under the wagon, this involuntary thought entered his mind and held fast. And he almost vented a groan of disbelieving self-anger as he considered it, recalling what somebody had said of him. Senalda? Pedro? Mr. Ree? He could not remember which one. Just the words: *A man such as this. If he wanted a woman. He would take her.*

It should have been true. So many of the finer qualities of humanity had been brutally stripped from him by harsh and bitter experience. He could take the life of a man without compunction. Why could he not take

112

the body of a woman without consideration for the object of his desire?

"Guess it just ain't your idea of a good time, feller," he told himself under his breath as he started to belly forward. "You just won't come unless you're invited."

It was the elderly Mason who was stretched out under his blankets closest to the wagon. Ned Fontaine and the youngster, Hardy, were nearby. Hardy was snoring loudly through a wide-open mouth. The other two breathed softly. Fontaine was smiling at a pleasant dream.

Edge eased up on to his haunches and raked his narrowed eyes over the camp site. He failed to spot his Winchester and guessed it was among the heap of saddles piled beside the quiet animals. The sleeping men had only the army issue Spencers close by where they lay.

He claimed the veteran's single-shot rifle without trouble. But Mason grunted and moved a hand as the Army Colt was slid from his holster, Edge probing under the blankets. Then the man settled back into peaceful sleep again.

The beaded sweat of tension became like pinpricks of icy needles against Edge's flesh. His pent-up breath was let out silently. The hammers of the two guns made sounds like shots as he cocked them. But only to his ears. No one else stirred.

He straightened to his full height and side-stepped around the group of sleeping men, Colt in his left hand and Spencer in his right, the stock of the rifle pressed against his side by an elbow.

Some of the horses whinnied as he neared them. A trooper moaned and rolled over onto his side. Edge swung the Colt, but the man did not wake.

Movement in another direction caught his eye. He

halted and tracked both guns, poised to fire and lunge for the cover of the heap of gear.

But he was covering Pedro Montez as the boy crawled out from the trees on the far side of the glade. The youngster froze and the moonlight showed the scowl on his face. Then there were other movements, ten feet to either side of the boy. His sister on the right and his mother on the left. They did not halt, but continued to inch towards the troopers. Pedro went with them.

Edge covered the final yard to the dumped saddles and crouched behind them. The guns in his hands shifted on the same back and forth shuttle as his eyes, watching for the first sign that the advance of the Montez family had been discovered.

There was sweat on his flesh again. The wife, son, and daughter of a blacksmith from a Mexican dirt farm village had no business closing in, unarmed, on a bunch of army deserters. They did not have what it took to succeed. Unless the will to win was enough.

They moved as silently as Edge had, like shadows in the moonlight. And disarmed three sleeping men with the same ease as if they were robbing corpses. Then they withdrew to the cover of the trees.

The horses, having accepted the presence of Edge, made further sounds of nervousness. The half-breed looked over his shoulder and saw the gowned figure of Ree crawling between the animals' legs. There was no trace of gentleness on his smooth-skinned face now. Just naked terror, which did not abate as he crouched beside Edge.

"Sir," he whispered. "The boy says he wishes to owe you nothing. Now that his father is dead, the wagon is his responsibility."

The half-breed nodded without expression, and

thrust the Colt at Ree. The Siamese took it by reflex action, but stared at it fearfully as Edge reached into the heap of gear and drew his Winchester from his own saddle boot.

"But I am a man of peace sir," the Oriental gasped. "I do not believe in violence."

"More than your illusion's about to be shattered, feller," Edge rasped.

Three rifle shots exploded against the mountain silence. The horses snorted and reared, flailing at their tethers. The oxen pawed at the grass. The sleeping forms of two men rolled and were still in death. Nine others screamed and cursed into awareness. All these reached for guns. Four failed to find them. Blankets were hurled aside and figures rose.

Three revolver shots cracked, less powerful than the opening volley and almost muted by the sounds of fury and panic vented from the gaping mouths of the deserters. Two more of them went to the ground and became inert. One was hit in the right kneecap and gave shrill, obscene voice to his agony.

"Over there!" Fontaine roared, and snapped off a shot into the trees, aiming wildly at the general area where all the survivors had seen the muzzle flashes of the Colts. "Charge the bastards!"

"You already took us for all we had, feller," Edge snarled, and exploded a bullet across the saddles.

The men with rifles fired them into the trees, then hurled them away and drew their Colts. Those whose guns had been stolen threw themselves to the ground and scampered towards the wagon.

One of those who tried this was hit in the side of the head by Edge's shot.

Those who had moved to obey Fontaine's order pulled up short and turned.

115

The half-breed fired again.

Two gunshots cracked out from the trees.

Another trooper died, hit in the stomach and chest.

Five of the deserters were left alive and one of these was writhing in agony, clutching at his blasted kneecap with both hands.

"Hold it!" Fontaine roared. "Friggin' hold the cruddin' shootin'!"

He and Hardy had their right hands fisted around the butts of Colts. The two other uninjured troopers had no guns. All four were in half crouches, fear and anger etched deep into their bristled faces as they swung their heads from the trees to the heap of saddles and back again. No man had had time to move more than six feet from the place where he had been sleeping.

The youthful Hardy got off one more shot after Edge and the Montez family had held their fire.

"I said to quit it, you crud!" Fontaine snarled, crashing down his free hand on the youngster's wrist.

As Hardy yelled in pain and the gun dropped from his hand, Fontaine tossed away his own Colt. Then he thrust his hands high into the air. The other three imitated him.

"And you can quit the stinkin' yellin', Dorcas!" the scar-faced man yelled.

The injured trooper moderated his sounds of agony to a low moaning.

"It's you people we took the lousy wagon from, ain't it?" Fontaine demanded, licking his lips between every second word. "Okay, we surrender! You can have it back!" He waved an arm to encompass the inert dead. "Didn't do these guys any good! We don't wanna finish up as bad as they are!"

Edge eased upright and stepped out from behind the

116

heap of gear. Ree stayed crouched and trembling in cover.

"Hey, man!" Fontaine said, a tremulous smile on his lips as he saw the move. And also saw the half-breed cant the Winchester to his shoulder. "We didn't kill you, did we? We could've but we didn't. Some wanted to, but I didn't let 'em, did I?"

"Your mistake, feller," Edge answered evenly, moving forward, ignoring the obvious survivors for long moments while he surveyed the sprawled forms, ensuring none were faking death. "Pretty sorry state it got you into."

Pedro and Isabella Montez moved into view, their colts leveled. Fontaine and the other troopers swung their attention to the twin brother and sister.

"Some wanted to take the girl," the scar-faced man went on. "I didn't allow that."

Isabella looked close to collapse. There was a glazed look in her dark eyes and her pulse raced at the side of her neck. Pedro was as calm and impassive as Edge.

"Why, *hombre?*" the boy asked evenly. "Why did you not kill us? Why did you not have your way with my sister?"

He sounded genuinely interested in having an answer. But Hardy read in Pedro's face the signs that this was not the end of the killing. Just a brief interlude.

"Because he's a fool, that's why!" the young trooper growled. "Same way we were fools to listen to him."

Pedro shifted the aim of the gun a fraction of an inch. The range was twenty feet and he proved he was a natural marksman. Hardy made no defensive move and took the bullet in the heart. He staggered back half a step, then corkscrewed to the ground. His dying silenced the moans of the injured man.

"Perhaps I will learn to be less of a fool if I listen to you, *hombre?*" Pedro offered.

Shock held the surviving troopers in open-mouthed silence. Isabella's reaction to the new death was a mere stilling and tightening of her trembling lips. Ree giggled.

"I just want outta the army," Fontaine said croakily. "All I wanted. And enough of a stake to set me up and safe. You just happened along. I figured just a— yeah, I'll be honest with you people. Just a bunch of Mexican peasants."

His hands were still above his head. He jerked out a thumb towards Edge. "Him, I knew was different. But he did me a favor blasting Sheldon. Kinda made things right for me. Showed me the gold and gave me the guts to kill those bastards Shotter and O'Keefe.

"But I had no reason to harm none of you people. You gave me the chance I been lookin' for. Lookin' for for years. And I blew it. It's a stinkin', cruddin' life."

"You have no need to be troubled by it further, *señor*." Isabella said flatly.

And shot Ned Fontaine.

The heavy Colt bucked in her double-handed grip. The bullet creased the trooper's shoulder. He yelled and started to turn. She cocked the hammer and fired again. This time she hit him in the hip and he went down on to one knee. His hands were thrust forward, his mouth wide.

Pedro fired four times, fanning the gun. A single bullet entered the eye of a trooper and the man was dead before he hit the ground. The other one had time to turn and run. Three wounds, widely spaced, blossomed patches of blood on his back.

Fontaine was dead by then, too. For the girl had learned to make allowances for the Colt's recoil. And

118

she placed a shot between his outstretched hands and into his screaming mouth.

Ree's giggling had expanded into harsh laughter. A sound similar to that which he had vented back in the saloon of the Dragonara Hotel in Amity Falls.

"You can't kill a helpless man!" the trooper with a bullet in his kneecap implored as Pedro advanced to stand over him.

The boy had realized the Colt was empty and stooped to pick up the one Fontaine had discarded. He stayed in the attitude as he aimed the gun at the last survivor of the deserters.

"Wounded, but still capable of thought, *hombre*," he said evenly as he pulled back the hammer. "You may still learn from the mistakes of other men. And there is still a long way to travel until we reach Mexico."

He squeezed the trigger. The wan face of the trooper was abruptly sprayed with the crimson which exploded from his left cheek. He became as still as the other corpses.

High overhead, the breeze which had been springing up and dying all night rustled the topmost branches of the trees.

"What was your plan, *hombre?*" Pedro asked as he dropped the Colt and straightened from his final kill.

"Stampede the horses and pick off the fellers that didn't get trampled. Figured I was single-handed."

The boy showed a grim smile. "The pupil has surprised his teacher."

"Didn't realize there were three in my class," Edge answered.

Only now did Isabella unclasp her hands and allow the gun to fall, then dropped her arms to her sides. Her breasts, the nipples still enlarged by the cold, were clearly defined in the moonlight.

119

"My mother and I insisted upon being part of this, *Señor* Edge," the girl said in a tone of infinite sadness, her glazed eyes fixed on the wagon parked beyond the sprawled and stiffening corpses of the troopers. "My mother paid for her insistence with her life."

She spoke slowly, with a pause between each distinctly articulated word. So that her brother had time to go back into the timber, pick up the body of his mother, and carry her towards the wagon before Isabella finished.

"The first shot they fired," Pedro added, showing no sign of his former exhaustion as he toted the corpse in both arms. She had taken a bullet in the center of her forehead. There was little blood around the hole. Her eyes were open and expressed determination.

"It is why I took human life," Isabella continued. "Not because of the gold. My father killed to protect this. My brother also. Perhaps my mother. Gold is like all material things. It can be replaced. Human life cannot. It can only be avenged."

The tears flowed. Her body jerked with sobs. She fell hard to her knees and then prostrated herself. Her weeping became silent.

Pedro rested the body of his mother on the grass while he lowered the tailgate of the wagon.

Edge shifted his cold, glinting gaze from the boy to the girl and knew that neither needed help.

"I must apologize for my apparent cowardice, sir," Ree said, emerging from behind the saddles as Edge started to pull his own gear from the heap. "And for the manner in which I am unable to control my most misplaced mirth in circumstances which are so tragic."

"You ain't yellow, feller?"

"Just the pigmentation of my skin, sir."

"And you don't really figure that death is funny?"

The Siamese looked from the impassive Edge to the weeping Isabella, to the grim-faced Pedro.

"Perhaps because I have never killed a fellow human being, sir," he suggested gently. "If I had, perhaps I would not find it impossible to—"

"No sweat, feller," the half-breed cut in. "Seems like ignorance really is bliss in your case."

"And it would seem that it is most folly to be wise in the ways of inflicting death," the Siamese replied, after making a second survey of the only other people left alive in the clearing. Then he changed his tone, as a sign that he was extemporizing his latest poem: "Death in numbers/Is no more distressing than/The passing of one/For when the hand of God/Reaches down to—"

"You want to hitch the team to the wagon?" Edge cut in wearily. "Be dawn pretty soon. You've a lousy odor, feller. But soon after sun up, there'll be a worse one from all these corpses."

Chapter Nine

THEY slept for the remainder of the night and until noon of the following day in a cave two miles south of the corpse-littered clearing on the shore of the lake. But, before bedding down, a fire was lit and they cooked and ate a meal. And felt warm and dry.

They awoke to the blistering heat of the day, not fully rested from the grueling, energy-sapping events of the previous one. They drank coffee and only Edge ate a meal—cold from his own supplies—before setting off again on the long journey towards Mexico.

The wagon was as it had been before the deserting troopers stole it, except that the bullet scar on the paintwork covering the gold strut had been camouflaged with a mixture of black wood ash and axle grease.

Inside, the space once occupied by the dying Antonio Montez was taken up by the blanket-wrapped corpse of his wife.

The half-breed and the boy rode their respective horses and both had reclaimed their own gear and weapons. Pedro had wanted to take a couple of the troopers' mounts as reserves for the mare and the gelding, but agreed sullenly with Edge that the army brand on the animals would invite trouble.

Isabella had criticized Mr. Ree with far more sever-

122

ity—in fact, had given him a snarling tongue-lashing when she spotted him robbing the dead of money and valuables. The Siamese's response had been a voluble and obsequious apology. But the girl was still aggrieved as the wagon rolled slowly through the rugged mountain country beneath the harsh afternoon sun, sitting as far away from the timid Oriental as she could on the wagon seat.

Not until they were back on the trail, far to the south of the valley entrance where the body of Antonio had been abandoned for scavengers, did anyone refer to the massacre in the clearing.

"We did wrong."

It was Isabella who made the comment, in a tone of grim determination. Edge was riding on the near side of the wagon, closest to her. Pedro was on the other side. Both looked at the girl, while Ree continued to concentrate on the trail ahead, the reins of the ox team held loosely in his hands. But it was he who responded to her.

"We have all sinned against our own God, madam. Perhaps I may talk of degree, as you have done. The soldiers had life and you took it. Even when it was not necessary. Life, the most cherished possession. After the breath was gone for their bodies, I merely took that which was of no more use to the lifeless."

There was no anger in his voice.

And Isabella ignored him. "Some were bad and perhaps deserved to die. But others were seeking only the same kind of relief we are attempting to bring in San Parral. Who are we to be judges of their mistaken methods? And their executioners?"

"They brought it upon themselves, *mi hermana!*" Pedro snapped. "And we did not do what we had to do only for San Parral. We did it for our dead parents."

123

He sat straighter in the saddle. "And we did it well." Now he leaned forward and turned his head to look across the front of the wagon at Edge. "Did we not prove ourselves most capable, *hombre?*"

The half-breed was rolling a cigarette. In completing this, and striking a match on the wagon, he maintained his constant vigilance over the surrounding terrain. "You did okay, kid," he allowed. "Just like those troopers made a fine job of stealing your gold. But best you remember where over-confidence got them."

"*Sí*, Pedro," his sister added. "And it ill becomes the son of Antonio Montez to boast of such things."

"I cannot help feeling the way I do," the boy countered, irritated. "Nor that I cannot be exactly as our father was." Abruptly, he smiled. "And I relish the taste of revenge. That makes me like you, eh, *hombre?*"

"If you live long enough, kid," Edge answered. "As the years pass, a man tends to lose his sweet tooth."

Isabella nodded, perhaps in agreement or maybe an outward sign of some secret and far removed thought.

There was just heat and dust and creaking timbers and clopping hooves for a long time. Then a stage coach approached from the south, the four-horse team hauling its burden at a steady canter. As the two vehicles passed, Isabella shouted a question. But the driver of the stage merely touched the brim of his hat, the guard raised a hand, and the passengers peered curiously out of the glassless windows.

"Either a town or a way station not far off," Edge supplied in answer to the girl's inquiry. "The team hitched to that stage is pretty fresh."

"Let us hope it is a town," she said with a sigh, "with people less bigoted than those of Amity Falls. With a Catholic priest who will bury my mother in consecrated ground."

124

Then she withdrew into her private realm of grief and remorse.

"*Hombre?*" Pedro called after another lengthy silence.

"Yeah, kid?"

"I have lost my interest in looking at the dead."

"So maybe you should take up knitting? Every youngster should have a hobby."

The boy showed an angry scowl, but then controlled the impulse. "Yes, I am young. But I seek the knowledge of experience. Jose Lajous was the first dead man I had ever seen. I have seen many since him."

"Sure, kid. After a while, every body gets to look the same. Dead ones, that is."

He glanced at the girl, but she was unaware of the narrowed, glinting blueness of his eyes as they surveyed her.

"Now it is the thoughts in a man's mind when he knows he is to die which intrigue me," Pedro insisted.

"Most fellers are happy to wait a long lifetime to find out about that, kid."

"But you thought my father was about to kill you, *hombre*. When you were tied to the wheel and he was aiming a gun at you. What was in your mind at that moment? Were you afraid? Did you have regrets of all you had left undone? Did you recall events in your life which—"

"Was thinking that stuff about a man dying with his boots on was crap, kid," the half-breed cut in, now dividing his attention between Isabella Montez and the huddled buildings of a town in the far distance. "That dying in bed has to be the best way to go—in the right company."

"*Hombre!*" Pedro snarled, realizing Edge was not

125

giving him a serious answer as he intercepted another appraising glance towards his sister. "There is something you should know! Isabella is promised to another man!"

"Ain't nothing easier to break than a promise, kid."

"The reason to do so would have to be very good indeed," the girl said, revealing that she had been aware of the exchange. There was no emotion in her tone as she continued to stare towards the town they were approaching.

"Nothing in the universe/Is all good/Or all bad/Even God/Has a mighty wrath." Having intoned his latest poem, Ree leaned forward to look around Isabella and smile at Edge. "I feel the madam—"

"No way, feller," Edge interrupted.

There was no town marker. The trail became a narrow street, lined by crudely built frame structures under the towering cliffs of a deep gorge. A sign over the stage depot proclaimed: MOUNTAIN CITY. There had been signs above other doorways, but the painted words had been obliterated by weather. As the wagon rolled along the street, it became obvious that Mountain City would have been a ghost town had it not been for the well-tended stage depot. Roofs had holes in them, windows were broken or boarded up and dust blown by old winds was heaped against firmly closed doorways. Cobwebs hung across stoops. The smell of the place was of ancient decay mixed with fresh horse droppings. The heat trapped between the high cliffs of the gorge was like that from an open oven door.

"Welcome, strangers! Ain't much of a town anymore, but everythin' the other side of this doorway is yours!"

The speaker was a gray-haired old-timer. He was six feet tall and broad at the shoulders and hips. He spoke

126

around a clay pipe clenched between false teeth. His tone was friendly, but his grip was tight on the frame and barrel of a Winchester slanted across his chest. He had stepped out of the shadows and onto the threshold of the stage depot.

"We are looking for a church and a priest, *señor*," Isabella responded, dejected as she peered around at the blank facades of the abandoned buildings.

"Never was neither here, ma'am. Just a bunch of miners and them that sponged off miners. All of them went when the vein give out. Just me left here. Takin' care of stage line horses and feedin' passengers."

There was a corral and barn beside the depot's main building. Four weary horses were in the corral.

"Miners die like other people, feller," Edge said.

The bearded old-timer nodded, puffing out blue, aromatic smoke from the pipe bowl. "Sure enough do, son. But the ones we had here weren't much for religion. About the only way you knew a funeral was happenin' was when folks took their hats off!"

He gave a cackling laugh.

"So the dead got buried?" Edge asked impassively.

"Sure did, son. Ain't healthy for the dead to—"

"In boxes?"

"Sure, Mort the mortician took care of that." He pointed with the Winchester. "Across the street there. 'Course, his name wasn't really Mort, but—"

Edge heeled the mare forward and the man in charge of the stage depot allowed his voice to trail away as the wagon moved in the wake of the half-breed. Then the old-timer watched with only mild interest as Edge and Pedro dismounted and, using their rifles, pried the boarding off a window of the undertaking parlor and climbed inside. They came out a minute later with a plain pine casket, hoisted it into the rear of the wagon and climbed aboard. They could be heard hammering down the lid nails with the butts of revolvers.

"Hey!" the old-timer yelled as the half-breed and the boy climbed out of the wagon and swung back into their saddles. "I oughta tell you folks! Take you more than three days to reach Cedarville, haulin' that rig! You could all catch the disease and die from totin' a corpse that long!"

"Obliged," Edge replied.

"I was only funnin' about you not bein' allowed in the depot, son! Why don't you get your buryin' done here? Then sit a spell! Have some coffee! Somethin' to eat, if you've a mind!"

"Mine's open, feller. But the lady's is set on a priest."

The bearded old man underwent another mercurial change of mood. "So frig off and leave a lonely old man to his empty day!" he snarled. "And I hope the Cedarville folks run you outta town when they smell what's in that box!"

"We go now, *señor!*" Isabella instructed Ree.

"*Sí*, move out!" Pedro added.

Edge glanced back at the old-timer, who was puffing furiously at his pipe. "Figure to keep the lid on it, feller," he called. "So mum's the word, uh?"

Shortly after sunup the following morning, the stench of decomposing flesh from inside the coffin got too strong to endure in the mounting heat of the new day. In a reversal of roles, Pedro had become much more of a realist than Isabella since they were orphaned. It was the boy who suggested that Senelda should be buried and he alone who convinced her to agree. He reminded her of her attitude about leaving the body of their father for the mountain scavengers—

128

that, like Antonio, their mother would not much care where her body rested if it were not possible to take it to San Parral.

There was a long-handled shovel among the wagon's equipment and Edge, Pedro, and Mr. Ree took turns at digging the grave in a hollow beneath a tree screened from the trail by an outcrop of rock.

Whether it was because of their grief—rekindled by the interment—or due to the fact that they had come to trust their traveling companions, the Montez twins remained out of sight behind the rock for a long time after the grave was filled in and marked, giving the half-breed and the Siamese ample opportunity to abandon them and steal the golden wagon if they were so inclined.

When the Mexicans emerged, their eyes were red-rimmed from spilled tears. But dry.

"We have decided that one day we will return to these mountains," Isabella announced when the wagon was rolling again, Edge and Pedro in their familiar out-rider positions. "To bring the bones of our father to this place and set them in the ground beside the resting place of our mother."

"It is a fine ambition, madam," Ree said.

"We think so." Her former chagrin towards the Siamese had disappeared.

"*Hombre?*" Pedro said after a while.

"Yeah, kid?"

"You could have taken the wagon. We could not have stopped you. I forgot a lesson. But it did not matter this time, eh?"

"You got lucky. It happens."

"It happens, also, that more than a body was buried just now," Ree suggested. "There is trust between all of us now?"

129

Isabella nodded. "If there can be that," she acknowledged, looking hard at Edge. "When there is a lack of understanding."

"I figure we understand each other, lady," the half-breed told her evenly. "It's just a matter of getting you to see things my way."

She showed a wan smile. "You have taught my brother well in your ways, Señor Edge. But he has been a willing pupil. It will be much more difficult for you to—"

"No sweat," the half-breed cut in on her with a smile that was almost warm. "You just ain't had his advantages."

"Advantages?"

"On the job training."

Chapter Ten

THERE was no rebuke from Pedro, and Isabella's response to the double-entendre was merely a long-suffering sigh.

The atmosphere of harmony remained with the wagon for more than ten days. On the trail through the San Juan Mountains. When the only other people they saw were at the widely spaced stage line way stations, in Cedarville and two other towns, and on the fields and pastures of isolated farms. The weather stayed fine, the heat getting more intense as they came down from the high country of the Colorado Plateau and headed across the northwestern corner of New Mexico Territory.

They replenished their supplies at town stores and farmsteads, but always made their night and noon camp in open country. The trouble which had begun north of Amity Falls and had dogged them relentlessly until they were south of Mountain City seemed a lifetime in the past.

There was a great deal of talk. About San Parral. About Montana. About Siam and China. And often there was laughter, for Mr. Ree could compose bad poetry on humorous subjects as well as serious ones.

Edge never volunteered information about his own past and he was never pressed on the subject. Once, while the wagon was rolling, Pedro taunted him good-humoredly about his endless surveillance of the empty country stretched out on all sides.

"Old habits die hard, kid," the half-breed had replied evenly. "Like a man who gets his in the back."

On another day, at noon camp while her brother and Mr. Ree attended to watering the animals, Isabella said, "You once told us that what waits at the end of the trail was your own business, Edge. At that time, you did not know what waited there, did you?"

"A life without any surprises in it must be pretty dull."

"San Parral is at the end of this trail. A few adobe houses, a church, a *cantina*, some fields, and lemon groves. Very dull for you. For me, home. And a handsome young boy named Luis who loves me and who I love in return. You make jokes, Edge. But inside you are a serious man, because you have been hurt often, I think?"

"Any time you want to see my scars, just let me know."

She responded to his grin by deepening her frown. "My brother and I owe you much. We can spare none of the gold to repay you. Pedro has nothing you want. I regret that what you desire of me cannot be given."

"Something else I told you a while back," Edge said, "That nothing's lost until it's been won."

She sighed deeply. "It is plain to me I am wasting my time in talking with you," she rasped, and whirled to move away, to start preparing the meal.

"Ain't nothing plain about you, Isabella," Edge had murmured, glinting eyes watching the sway of her body and the way the sunlight added a sheen to her swinging hair.

It was three days after this exchange, as they neared

132

the Mission of Santa Christobel on the southern bank of the Chaco River, that the long interlude of peace was violently shattered.

There was a hot wind blowing from the east, billowing dust and tumbleweed out of the mouth of Chaco Canyon and hurling the debris high and wide across the open country spread to either side of the dried-up river bed.

But they had seen the yellow adobe buildings of the mission—a high-towered church and three other buildings skirting a courtyard—before the thick dust drew a choking veil across the scene. And they made for the shelter of the mission, kerchiefs pulled up over their nostrils and mouths and eyes narrowed against the stinging motes.

Visibility was only a few feet and every sound was blanketed by the howl and hiss of the wind. The animals were skittish, but the horses responded to the calming influence of expert riders. Mr. Ree had more trouble controlling the ox team, until Edge leaned down from one side and Pedro the other to take hold of the traces and steer the nervous animals on a direct route to the mission.

The courtyard was entirely enclosed by the buildings, except for a gateway just wide enough to admit the wagon. The double gates were invitingly open and, once the wagon was inside, Edge and Pedro swung fast from their saddles and ran back to close them.

The strong, hot, dust-laden wind fought their efforts every inch of the way. And their muscles were not relieved of strain until Mr. Ree joined them and slid a stout plank through two iron brackets to keep the gates securely fastened.

The noise of the storm did not abate. But they were sheltered from the direct force of the stinging, choking

133

dust. For the wind lost power after curling over the gates and the roofs of the buildings. The dust continued to swirl and eddy, though, like a restlessly moving gray curtain hung across the buildings surrounding the courtyard.

Edge opened the door closest to the gateway and stepped into a small schoolroom furnished with crudely made but neatly aligned furniture. Wind-borne dust danced in the hot air, growing thicker by the moment until he had crossed the room and fastened shutters over the two glassless windows.

The dust settled on a dirt floor, twenty desks and chairs suitable for children, a larger desk and chair at one end of the room, a blackboard on an easel and two free-standing closets. Most of the pictures which had once been pinned to the walls were now scattered across the floor. Those which had been sheltered from the main blast of the wind were obviously drawn and painted by young hands. Indian.

"Where are the children?" Isabella asked as she entered the schoolroom and gazed around, puzzled and a little afraid.

"Maybe it's July Fourth," Edge replied.

"What?"

"Or some other holiday. Where's Pedro and the reason poetry's a dying art form?"

"Taking the animals to the stables. I remember this place from when we came north. We spent a night here. It is run by Mexicans. For the Indians. Apaches, Utes, and Navahos. There is the mission church. This school. A house for Father Ramon and the three men who assist him. And a stable. All seem to be as deserted as here. I do not like it."

"We're stuck with it until the storm blows out," Edge told her, pulling the kerchief off his lower face.

She imitated his action—even with half her face its natural color and the other half stained by sweat-pasted dust she was startlingly beautiful. The half-breed found her more appealing than ever, perhaps because the final vestiges of girlhood had been stripped from her by the harrowing events along the violent trail they had traveled. Now, she had the face of a full-grown woman to match her body. And, despite the fact that in chronological terms she had aged only a few weeks and was still almost young enough to be his daughter, Edge felt suddenly easier in his mind.

Because a burden of guilt had been lifted? Had it really been self-reproach which had set his behavior pattern towards Isabella Montez? The thought that he was some kind of monstrous ogre lusting after the in-nocent flesh of a child?

But then he met her wide eyes and saw the fear in them, a much deeper fear than the nervousness she had experienced when she first entered the schoolroom. And he knew that he was the reason for this new ter-ror—that the glittering eyes under the hooded lids and the way his lips were curled back from his teeth made her terribly afraid of him.

In that moment, as both of them realized it was the first time they had been alone together since they met, she was suddenly a young child again. Despite the re-cently matured face and the fully developed body, Isa-bella Montez was a young girl who had caused him no harm. And had suffered enough.

"*Señor* Edge?" she whispered hoarsely.

"No sweat, kid," he told her, crossing the dusty room and being careful to swing wide of her. "Stay here while I check out the place."

Had the moment of terror not been, perhaps she would have insisted on staying close to him. But she

135

nodded gratefully as he pulled open the door. Then, as she was about to sit down at a desk of one of the absent Indian children, a smile of shining happiness spread across her lovely face.

"Luis!" she exclaimed. "*Mi*—"

Edge was half turned towards her. As he saw the smile and heard her words, a movement scratched at the periphery of his vision. Confusion replaced her smile. There was a gunshot—away from the schoolroom—the sound of it muted by the noise of the storm.

The half-breed felt the familiar tight ball of cold fear at the pit of his stomach. And received a fleeting glimpse of the man outside the doorway before the muzzle of a rifle hit him in the stomach and the taut fear became white-hot agony, which exploded and sent searing heat to every nerve ending in his body. He was folding forward then, and the effort of channeling all his strength to his legs prevented him from getting a hand to his holstered Colt. Through eyes misted by the tears of pain, he saw a pair of scuffed boots set firmly on the dusty ground of the courtyard. The stock of the rifle crushed his hat and it was as if he wore no hat and was bald. The impact of the blow had, to his own ears, the sound of another gunshot, much closer. He was certain his skull was cracked open and that the liquid contents of his head were gushing out. More agony than he had ever felt before. Then nothing. No sense of falling. Just the pitch darkness of a deep mine.

"I am sorry for the shock, Isabella," Luis Porrero said across the form of the half-breed crumpled on the threshold. "Three years is a long time. There are changes. People change. You will come outside."

He was about twenty. Tall and slender, with a strong-featured, good-looking face. His clothes were old and worn and poor quality. But his crossed-bandoliers, double-holstered gunbelt, two Colt revolvers, and Winchester rifle were all new.

"You are now a bandit?" the girl gasped, her wide-eyed gaze moving between the unconscious Edge and the face of the boy she had planned to marry.

"If you do not come outside, I will kill you where you stand," Luis warned. "To prove myself fully to my new friends."

She hesitated only a moment, all her attention concentrated on the handsome face. Then she saw that he meant what he said and she went to the doorway. She turned sideways, to squeeze over the threshold around the slumped half-breed.

The hot wind out of Chaco Canyon was losing power. There was less noise and the dust inside the surrounding adobe buildings was beginning to settle on the courtyard.

"You have killed him!" she accused dully. "He was a good—"

"To me, he was nothing!" Luis interrupted, and gestured with the rifle for her to walk ahead of him.

In his dark eyes now there was an expression not far removed from the look which Edge had directed at her a few moments ago. When she could not see him, and his eyes roved over her from the rear, his lust expanded.

"Why?" she asked.

"Did I become a bandit?" he countered.

"That, too."

She saw Pedro and only now, when relief flooded through her, did she recall the shot which had coincided with the opening of the schoolroom door.

"Because I want more than San Parral can offer me," Luis answered. "And a larger share of the gold you bring."

"Gold?"

Pedro was emerging from the stable, his hands clasped on top of his hatless head, a rifle in the hands of another bandit nudging him in the back.

"Did your father not tell of the letter he wrote to my father, Isabella?"

"Letter?"

"He did not. My father died from the fever last year. I opened the letter. Your father wrote he was coming home to San Parral. With his wife and you and your brother. And much gold to make life good for the village. He wrote that preparations should be made for the wedding. He wanted to surprise you, I suppose."

The wind and the dust were now completely gone. The sky was blue again and the blistering sun shone with bright intensity on the Mission of Santa Christobel. Pedro and Isabella were being guided across the courtyard towards the arched entrance of the church. Four men stood in the shade of the porchway—Father Ramon and two others in clerical garb, and a third bandit. The priest and his assistants had their hands tied behind their backs and were gagged by filthy rags.

"We have been betrayed," Isabella told Pedro as they came together at the center of the courtyard. "By—"

"I have seen him," Pedro answered flatly, still expressing the same brand of hatred which had spread across his face when he first saw and recognized Luis.

The bandit who had captured him was ten years older than Luis. He had a flabby build and a round, heavy-jowled face.

The man who stood behind the bound prisoners was about fifty. His build was big, but solid. He had a moustache and beard, neatly trimmed, and a gold ring at his right ear. Both men were dressed in a similar

138

manner to Luis and were armed in the same way. Luis had a *sombrero* on his head while the other two allowed their headgear to hang down their backs.

"One of the holy men is missing, Alberto." Pedro's captor said. "The signal shot?"

Alberto shrugged. "Hold still," he told Father Ramon, and leaned his Winchester against the prisoner, stock on the ground and muzzle to the priest's rump. He took out a cigar and lit it. "Bullets are expensive. Why be wasteful, Felipe?"

The Montez twins were ordered to halt, fifteen feet in front of the other three prisoners. From this close, Isabella and Pedro could see the shock in the eyes of Father Ramon and his helpers and the tracks of their tears across their cheeks.

Alberto was smiling as he spoke. Now, as he blew out blue tobacco smoke, his expression became grim. "The father, Luis?"

"It was not *Señor* Montez," Luis replied. "A *gringo* I never saw before."

The cruel eyes of Alberto switched from Isabella to Pedro and back again. "Well?"

Pedro was tacitly defiant. Isabella had looked pityingly at the priest, then glanced about the courtyard, her eyes seeking the little Siamese.

"Just us!" Alberto snarled.

Isabella looked fearfully at him. "The man is a friend who has helped us," she supplied, having difficulty speaking the words. "My father is dead. My mother, too. One killed by Indians. The other by American soldiers."

The obvious leader of the bandits nodded and vented a sigh of satisfaction. "It is good. Like I say, bullets are expensive. Two we save."

Isabella gasped at the callousness of the men. Pedro

dropped his hands from his head and curled one arm around the shoulders of his sister.

"Do not torment us!" he snarled at Alberto. "If you intend to kill us, do it now!"

Alberto was holding the cigar to his lips. He blew out another stream of smoke, then drew one of his Colts. His action was smooth and fast. Isabella screamed and felt her brother become rigid with terror.

The revolver bucked in the bandit's hand. He drew calmly against the cigar. The bullet cracked between Father Ramon and one of his helpers and tore into Pedro's chest. The boy took a backward step, his arms falling to his sides. Blood blossomed into a large stain on his shirt front and he went down, curling into a fetal position. His sister's scream reached a shrill peak and was curtailed. She crouched down beside the boy.

Alberto slid the revolver back into its holster and continued to smoke. "He asked and I gave, *señorita*," the bandit said evenly. "We owe a favor to the Montez family. To your father, for writing of the gold to Luis. But your father can be given no more. So it is his son who collects."

"You are animals!" Isabella tried to shriek. But her words emerged at the level of a hushed whisper as she raked her gaze around the impassive faces of the three bandits.

Alberto clenched the cigar between his tobacco-stained teeth and picked up his Winchester. He took two backward steps, into the deep shade of the porch. But the sunlight could still reach the barrel of the rifle as he leveled it.

"No!" the girl exclaimed, and this time her voice was loud. The single word as she sprang erect echoed between the facades of the surrounding buildings.

The priest and his two assistants expressed pity for her.

The clicks of the rifle's lever action being pumped had a dry sound.

The gun exploded and belched death.

Father Ramon fell forward. The two other men in clerical garb showed their terror. The action was pumped and the trigger squeezed. Then again.

Still in line, the three prisoners were stretched out full length in the dusty courtyard face down and wrists tied behind their backs. At the nape of the neck of each of them there was a small hole, at the crowns of their heads, much larger holes. Their hair was soaked with crimson blood.

Isabella dropped to her knees and crossed herself.

"The *gringo* is dead?" Alberto asked.

"He is human," Luis replied, just as calmly. "So he does not have a head of iron."

"Good. You will do what you wanted. Felipe and I will find the gold."

He rested his Winchester against the porch wall and gestured for the fat bandit to join him. They ambled casually across the sun-bright courtyard to where the wagon was parked just inside the closed gateway, the oxen still in the traces.

"You will take off your clothes, Isabella," Luis Perrero said softly.

The girl was still on her knees, hands clasped, eyes closed and lips moving to form the words of a prayer. The demand of the boy she had loved shocked her into speechless paralysis.

"Since my father died and I was left to scratch at the dusty soil of San Parral, I wanted to become a bandit," Luis said. "Do as I tell you, Isabella. Stand up and do

141

it. Or I will shoot you in each ankle and strip you myself."

She could move now. Turn and look at him. See him lower the aim of the rifle. See from his face that he was ready to carry out the threat. She stood up. She smelled the sweat of her body. The scene in the blisteringly hot, dusty dry courtyard blurred. She struggled against the threat of a faint, and began to unbutton her shirt with trembling fingers.

"But I had nothing to offer the bandit group of Alberto Bravo. When I went to them, they beat me and sent me back to San Parral. Then I received the letter from your father to my father."

She drew the shirt off her shoulders. Beneath it was a white chemise, stained dark by sweat. She began to unfasten her pants at the waist. Her large breasts were firm, trembling with each movement she made.

"Then, the group did not beat me. They listened and agreed to my plan that we should wait here for your wagon. Do not all the people of San Parral who come to the United States stop here at the mission? I knew you would come here."

She pushed her pants down over her legs, then had to sit and take off her boots first. Her underwear was all in one, covering her from ankles to chest. There were button fastenings from the top hem to her midriff. She was trembling less violently now. She stared at the wagon, as the men inside began to toss out its contents. But she showed no interest in what was happening.

"We waited to the north of here," Luis went on, his dark eyes shining brighter as he watched the girl's full body being uncovered. "When we saw you coming in the far distance, we came to the mission. We sent the Indian children back to the reservation and we took

142

the priests prisoner. Then we waited for you as the dust storm came.

"So now I am really a bandit, Isabella. Trusted by Alberto Bravo. And allowed to have that which I most regretted losing when I made my decision. You."

Every item of the girl's clothing was removed now, heaped untidily at her feet. She stood rigidly erect, arms at her sides. Every olive-brown plane at the front of her body was revealed to the burning gaze of Luis; her shoulders, her large, slightly sagging breasts, her stomach, her thighs, the flesh smooth and firm—the nipples cresting her breasts and the triangle of luxuriant hair arrowing down at the base of her belly providing the only areas of faintly contrasting coloration.

"You will lie down and spread yourself for me, Isabella," the young bandit said, his voice croaking with passion. "Out here in the open. On the dust with the sun on you. In the life I have chosen, there is no place for the luxuries of privacy and comfort."

The girl's expression suggested she was in a world removed from the scene of death and lust happening around her. But she could hear his words and she complied.

Luis allowed the Winchester to fall from his shaking hands and took two forward steps to stand between the splayed and naked legs of the unmoving girl. He unfastened his pants and groped into the opening to expose his thrusting want before he dropped to his knees.

The sweat had dried on Isabella's body. But there was wetness on her face as she spilled tears for what might have been. Then she vented a moan of pain and revulsion as Luis guided himself into her. The blood of her lost virginity was on his hands as they clawed at her breasts. His breath was hot on the flesh of her neck as he sighed his release.

143

Neither he, nor Isabella, nor Alberto Bravo and Felipe saw a hand reach out from the shaded interior of the church to claim the rifle leaning against the porch wall.

Likewise, nobody saw Edge move slightly as he regained consciousness.

The half-breed was awash on a sea of agony. But he did not cry out. His right cheek was pressed against the threshold of the schoolroom doorway. When his eyes cracked open, his vision was blurred. It cleared and he received a tilted view of the scene in the courtyard. Four slumped figures with flies feeding on congealing blood. A fully clothed man thrusting his lust into the naked body of the girl. Items of the wagon's freight being hurled out over the tailgate. The sounds of the scene comprised the panting of one man and the cursing of two others.

"Luis! There is no gold here!"

Alberto and Felipe jumped down from the rear of the wagon. Luis reached a frenetic climax and emptied himself into Isabella. The girl groaned, and her body spasmed as vomit gushed from her mouth.

Luis wrenched out of her and leapt upright, revulsion changing to terror as he whirled and saw the angry Alberto striding towards him. His pants were still open to show his shrinking flesh splashed with the blood of Isabella.

Edge withdrew into the schoolroom and his vision became misted again as he clawed himself upright against the wall. Flies buzzed away from the crushed, blood-soaked crown of his hat. He felt for his gun and his hand fisted around the butt jutting from the holster.

Cold anger struggled against searing agony. And won. He could hear voices outside in the courtyard speaking Mexican, the words indistinct. He went away from them, between the neat rows of dusty desks. His rage was entirely directed inwards for allowing himself to be taken by the young Mexican. Maybe later there would be some to spare for what had happened to Isabella Montez.

Silently, he opened the shutters at one of the windows and climbed outside.

"If all this is for nothin—" Alberto snarled, halting in front of Luis as the youngster fastened his pants.

"There is gold! I will make her tell where! I swear it, Alberto!"

"So talk to her! Not me!"

Alberto Bravo stood with a hand fisted around each of his holstered Colts. The fat Felipe was beside him, Winchester held across his chest. Luis turned to glare down at the naked, still spread-eagled girl. He was now more afraid than she was.

"Isabella! The gold! Where did you leave the gold?"

"If I do not tell you?" she whispered, her vomit-run lips hardly moving. "What will you do to me? Kill me?"

Luis reached to draw one of his Colts.

Alberto reached out an arm and thrust the boy aside. "Stupid! If you kill her—Listen, bitch!" He crouched between her splayed legs, clawed both hands and fastened them hard over the mounds of her already bruised breasts. "We have already spent much money by shooting bullets. They brought quick death. To kill you slowly will cost nothing. And we will still be rich with gold. Because you will tell us where you hid it. You understand, bitch?"

He squeezed her flesh, his filthy fingernails digging in hard enough to break the skin and draw tiny spurts of blood.

Isabella screamed. Louder than ever before. It rang

145

between the implacable facades of the surrounding buildings like a sound compounded of all the agony, misery, and desperation in the world. And did not stop until Alberto Bravo dropped a knee and thudded it into the girl's crotch. She gasped as he eased the pressure of his hands.

"Yes, I think you understand. You will tell now? Then one bullet. Very quick."

Edge had made a half circuit of the mission and climbed in through a window of the stable. The Winchester from the boot of his still saddled black mare was in his hands.

"It is on the wagon," Isabella gasped, then gagged as more bile rose from her throat into her mouth. "The metal, it is not all iron. Much is gold, painted to look like—"

"Stay here, stupid!" Alberto snarled as Luis matched the whirling movement of himself and Felipe.

The youngster obeyed, looking cowed, as the other two bandits ran towards the parked wagon.

"The fields and house of your father were not much," Isabella gasped. "But you were master of them."

"Be quiet!" Luis snarled.

"What will you do? Kill me? Without the permission of that other animal who leads you?"

"Shut your filthy mouth!" He took two strides and drew back a foot to launch a kick at her head.

She flinched instinctively.

"It is here!" Felipe yelled in high excitement. "Under the paint! Like she said!"

Luis froze in the kicking attitude.

"Kill her, boy!" Alberto called. "Quick, so we can leave!"

146

Edge stepped out into the sunlight, pumping the action of the Winchester.

A shot exploded from high up.

Edge, Isabella, and the three bandits looked towards the top of the church tower. Mr. Ree was up there, standing in a broad aperture. A Winchester was aimed from his shoulder and he was steadying himself with his back against the big bell.

His bullet went wide of the target and dug up a divot of dusty dirt ten feet away from Luis.

"One we did not see!" Felipe yelled, bringing his own rifle to the aim.

Alberto and Luis went for their Colts.

Edge shot Luis. He fired from the hip and Isabella screamed and rolled clear as the young Mexican was knocked forward and down, blood staining the back of his shirt and gushing from the exit wound in his chest.

"And one with a head of iron!" Alberto snarled.

He and Felipe whirled, ignoring Ree as the Siamese sent another shot downwards and hit one of the oxen in the wagon traces. The animal fell heavily, without a sound of pain.

Edge turned from the waist and levered the action of the rifle. He squeezed the trigger and his bullet took Felipe in the neck. The fat bandit staggered backwards, hurling away his Winchester and flinging both hands to the bloody hole in his flesh. His skull made a dry sound as he fell and his head was split open on a wheel rim. What flowed out was very wet.

Alberto had both Colts leveled at Edge. His fingers were taut against the triggers, the knuckles white. The half-breed was in the process of pumping the action again.

Ree fired and the bullet dug adobe out of the school-room wall.

147

Isabella squeezed the trigger of Luis's Winchester. Alberto was hit in the stomach and folded forward. Both his guns exploded, and the bullets drilled into the dirt of the courtyard. The rifle in Edge's hands belched another bullet. The top of the bandit's head fountained blood. He whipped erect, then fell backwards, rigid for a moment. Then limp.

The girl was prone now, her exposed back caked with dust made wet by her sweat. She released the rifle and came up onto all fours, then gathered her clothes, covered herself as much as she was able, stood up, and sprinted for the privacy of the shaded church interior.

Edge rested his rifle against the stable wall and took off his hat to grimace at the dried blood on the crushed crown. He explored the crusting on his skull.

"Sir!" the Siamese called down from the top of the tower as Edge winced at the pain triggered by his probing fingers. "I have never fired a gun before today."

Edge reshaped his hat, replaced it on his head, and squinted up at Ree, narrowed eyes glinting out of the shadow of the brim. "It showed, feller!"

"But I was of assistance to you, was I not?" He sounded proud.

"Always a help to have a highly-placed friend." He beckoned. "You want to come on down now?"

"So that we may all finish the journey to San Parral?" Isabella asked from inside the church. She sounded breathless. From her experience, or perhaps merely with the effort of hurriedly donning her clothes. "The best I could give to a man is now gone, *señor*. But, if you are still—"

"About time you learned not to make plans for the future," Edge cut in.

"No!" the girl screamed.

The single, shrill word cut across the intoning voice of the Siamese poet.

"When the past has been so full/With trials and pains and death/Perhaps the future is————."

Edge whirled, arms snaking out and hands clawed to snatch up his rifle.

The bell at the top of the tower clanged. Ree had been standing unsupported, speaking the lines to the barren terrain stretching out to either side of the dried-up River Chaco. The swinging bell hit the back of his thighs and tipped him off the narrow ledge.

He screamed once, then was silent. Perhaps claimed by merciful unconsciousness as he plummeted downwards, his gown billowing in the hot slipstream and his flat hat scaling off his head. His falling form turned over twice, almost gracefully. Then he hit the courtyard. Dust billowed around him. His flesh was burst open by the impact. Blood sprayed out on all sides. Bones broke. He was still and the dust settled, adhering to the crimson wetness soaking through his gown. The flies swarmed in to feed.

"Father Ramon's third helper!" Isabella Montez moaned as she advanced slowly from the church, fully dressed now. "He lived after he was shot. He tried to rise. His hands were bound at his back. But he was able to use them. To try to pull himself up. On the bell rope."

She was out in the bright sun now, on the corpse-littered courtyard of the Mission of Santa Christobel. But she looked only at the shattered, burst-open remains of the last man to die, then covered her eyes with her hands.

"How horrible!"

"He's a mess now, sure enough," Edge muttered,

canting the rifle to his shoulder. "But he looked real good coming down."

Isabella began to weep, and staggered across to kneel beside her brother's corpse. Before turning to get the horses from the stable, the half-breed allowed his glinting eyes to travel from the top of the bell tower to the body at its base. Then, "Yeah," he murmured. "Poet Ree in motion."

the Executioner

**The gutsiest, most exciting hero in years.
Imagine a guy at war with the Godfather
and all his Mafioso relatives! He's rough,
he's deadly, he's a law unto himself —
nothing and nobody stops him!**

THE EXECUTIONER SERIES by DON PENDLETON

Order		Title	Book #	Price
_____	# 1	WAR AGAINST THE MAFIA	P401	$1.25
_____	# 2	DEATH SQUAD	P402	$1.25
_____	# 3	BATTLE MASK	P403	$1.25
_____	# 4	MIAMI MASSACRE	P404	$1.25
_____	# 5	CONTINENTAL CONTRACT	P405	$1.25
_____	# 6	ASSAULT ON SOHO	P406	$1.25
_____	# 7	NIGHTMARE IN NEW YORK	P407	$1.25
_____	# 8	CHICAGO WIPEOUT	P408	$1.25
_____	# 9	VEGAS VENDETTA	P409	$1.25
_____	#10	CARIBBEAN KILL	P410	$1.25
_____	#11	CALIFORNIA HIT	P411	$1.25
_____	#12	BOSTON BLITZ	P412	$1.25
_____	#13	WASHINGTON I.O.U.	P413	$1.25
_____	#14	SAN DIEGO SIEGE	P414	$1.25
_____	#15	PANIC IN PHILLY	P415	$1.25
_____	#16	SICILIAN SLAUGHTER	P552	$1.25
_____	#17	JERSEY GUNS	P328	$1.25
_____	#18	TEXAS STORM	P353	$1.25
_____	#19	DETROIT DEATHWATCH	P419	$1.25
_____	#20	NEW ORLEANS KNOCKOUT	P475	$1.25
_____	#21	FIREBASE SEATTLE	P499	$1.25
_____	#22	HAWAIIAN HELLGROUND	P625	$1.25
_____	#23	ST. LOUIS SHOWDOWN	P687	$1.25
_____	#24	CANADIAN CRISIS	P779	$1.25
_____	#25	COLORADO KILL-ZONE	P824	$1.25
_____	#26	ACAPULCO RAMPAGE	P868	$1.25

and more to come . . .

TO ORDER

Please check the space next to the book/s you want, send this order form
together with your check or money order, include the price of the book/s
and 25¢ for handling and mailing to:

**PINNACLE BOOKS, INC. / P.O. Box 4347
Grand Central Station / New York, N.Y. 10017**

☐ **CHECK HERE IF YOU WANT A FREE CATALOG**
I have enclosed $_____check_____or money order_____
as payment in full. No C.O.D.'s.

Name_____

Address_____

City_____State_____Zip_____
Please allow time for delivery)

PB-38

Violence is a man! His name is Edge...

The bloodiest action-series ever published, with a hero who is the meanest, most vicious killer the West has ever seen.

It's sharp — It's hard — It's EDGE

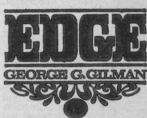

GEORGE G. GILMAN

Order		Title	Book #	Price
_____	# 1	THE LONER	P596	$1.25
_____	# 2	TEN GRAND	P703	$1.25
_____	# 3	APACHE DEATH	P667	$1.25
_____	# 4	KILLER'S BREED	P597	$1.25
_____	# 5	BLOOD ON SILVER	P598	$1.25
_____	# 6	RED RIVER	P668	$1.25
_____	# 7	CALIFORNIA KILL	P599	$1.25
_____	# 8	HELL'S SEVEN	P750	$1.25
_____	# 9	BLOODY SUMMER	P293	$ .95
_____	#10	BLACK VENGEANCE	P333	$ .95
_____	#11	SIOUX UPRISING	P600	$1.25
_____	#12	DEATH'S BOUNTY	P669	$1.25
_____	#13	THE HATED	P560	$1.25
_____	#14	TIGER'S GOLD	P624	$1.25

AND MORE TO COME . . .

TO ORDER

Please check the space next to the book/s you want, send this order form together with your check or money order, include the price of the book/s and 25¢ for handling and mailing, to:

**PINNACLE BOOKS, INC. / P.O. Box 4347
Grand Central Station / New York, N.Y. 10017**

☐ **Check here if you want a free catalog.**

I have enclosed $_____ check_____ or money order_____
as payment in full. No C.O.D.'s.

Name_____

Address_____

City_____ State_____ Zip_____
(Please allow time for delivery)